NASHVILLE PUBLIC LIBRARY

FOUNDATION

*This book
made possible
through generous gifts
to the
Nashville Public Library
Foundation Book Fund*

NPLF.ORG

The
TRACKS

Written by

ROSALYN RIKEL RAMAGE

Order this book online at www.trafford.com
or email orders@trafford.com

Most Trafford titles are also available at major online book retailers.

Printed in the United States of America.

ISBN: 978-1-4269-9271-1 (sc)
ISBN: 978-1-4269-9272-8 (e)

Library of Congress Control Number: 2011914976

Trafford rev. 09/14/2011

 www.trafford.com

North America & international
toll-free: 1 888 232 4444 (USA & Canada)
phone: 250 383 6864 ♦ fax: 812 355 4082

For my children,
Rae Ellyn, Ron, and Risa

* * * * * * *

Special thanks are extended to the many family members as well as old and new friends who have been involved in various ways to help bring this book into existence. Specific acknowledgement is given to students at Barfield Elementary School, Eakin Elementary School, and DuPont Hadley Middle School, as they especially encouraged me to share my story. But without the support and encouragement of my husband, Don, this book would never have been written or published.

THE FAMILY (Photograph Circa 1914)
Front Row: Frederick, William, Arthur
Middle Row: Papa, Edward, Mama
Back Row: Emma Mae and Clarence

Mini-Glossary of German Words Used in the Story:

German Word:	Pronunciation:	Meaning:
Auf Weidersehen	(auf-vee-dair-zane)	Goodbye
Danke	(dahn-kuh)	Thank you
Fraulein	(froy-lain)	Young lady
Gesundheit	(geh-soont-hyt)	Good health,

but sometimes used as the expression for
"Bless you," especially following a sneeze!

Guten Morgen	(goot-en mor-gen)	Good morning
Gute Nacht	(goot-eh nakht)	Good night
Guten Tag	(goot-en tahk)	Good day
Ja	(yah)	Yes
Junger Mann	(yoon-geh man)	Young man
Mutter	(muht-er)	Mother
Nein	(nine)	No

CHAPTER 1

"Watch out for Bossy!" I hollered at Edward as he led the cows to the barn for milking. "She's coming up behind you with her head down!"

Instantly, my ten-year-old brother turned around, flung his hands in the air, and yelled, "Hey!"

Bossy stopped in her tracks. She glared at him, shaking her head resentfully.

"Thanks for the warning, Emma Mae," Edward called back as he moved off the cow path. "She was really after me that time."

Bossy had a reputation for sneaking up behind people and giving them nudges with her horns. Now that she had been stopped, she led the other cows to the barn where Edward had their food waiting for them in the milking stalls. Papa and our older brother Clarence were due back any time now from working in the fields with the team of horses.

I jumped down from the top of the gate where I was sitting and sprinted across the barn lot to join Edward. "Since I've finished feeding the chickens and gathering the eggs, would you like me to help feed the pigs?" I asked him.

"Why don't you take care of the horses' feed and I'll take care of the pigs? Then we'll be done."

"Good idea," I said in my most agreeable twelve-year-old voice. I hurried into the larger section of the barn and opened the barrel where we stored the horses' feed. When I finished filling the wooden troughs, I got the pitchfork and tossed some fresh hay into the stalls. As I put the pitchfork up and walked out of the barn, I sneezed. That was my usual reaction to being around hay.

"*Gesundheit*," Edward yelled from the pigpen, laughing. That's the German expression for "bless you," which our family frequently said when somebody sneezes. Our ancestors migrated to Kentucky from Germany many years earlier; but even now, in 1914, we still sprinkled some German words and phrases through our conversation.

Ed emptied the slop bucket full of dishwater and table scraps into the pigs' trough. He added some dry food to this mixture to finish out the pigs' supper.

I climbed the fence that separated the barn lot from the back yard. The last tinge of orange was almost gone from the clouds. "If we're going to the hideout to get my crown for tonight's party before dark, we'd better get going," I called to Edward.

"I'm ready when you are," he announced, jumping the fence and running to my side. He plopped the empty slop bucket on the back steps beside the basket of eggs I had gathered earlier. He put his hands in the hip pockets of his overalls as he looked at the darkening sky.

"Can we get across the tracks and back before dark?" I asked.

Edward scratched above his left ear like he always did when he wasn't sure about something.

"*Ja!*" he answered. "I think we can make it if we hurry."

"Since I need the crown for part of my costume, let's go!"

With that, we took off running like the wind, our bare feet skimming along the pathway. We ran through the garden gate, past the sweet potato cellar, and toward the nearby railroad tracks. Then we took the familiar trail that led across the tracks, up the small incline, and into the wooded area beyond.

It was getting quite dusky in the woods by now, but we could still see the path that led to the clump of bushes that was our hideout. "Wait, Ed," I whispered as we stopped beside the thicket. I grabbed his arm. "Why do I have prickly shivers running up and down my spine? I've got that weird feeling that something strange is about to happen."

"I feel it, too," he whispered. "Probably because it's getting so dark here in the woods."

I shrugged my shoulders. "Maybe so. Let me grab my crown and I'll race you back to the house."

This cluster of low-growing bushes looked like a solid mass from the outside, but it hid a wonderful clearing in the middle. A small opening in one side is what we used for the entrance. I dropped down on my hands and knees and crawled in the open space.

"It's almost dark inside here," I said in a hushed tone. I could hardly see the doll bed on the other side of the clearing. Edward had made the bed out of pieces of scrap lumber, and I had filled it with straw.

There on the small bed was my China doll I had also left in the hideout yesterday. "Hello, Maizey," I whispered to her. "You look funny with my paper crown on your little head." The doll's eyes in her tiny porcelain face stared back at me. "I'm going to wear this crown to a party tonight. A *Halloween* party. I'm so excited!"

I picked her up and pecked a kiss on her cheek before plopping her back down on her bed. "Thanks for trying out my crown, Maizey. See you tomorrow."

Quickly, I jerked around to crawl back out of the opening, but I bumped into something that yelled. My heart lurched!

"Watch out, Emma Mae!" Edward hollered. "Don't knock me down!"

I laughed out loud. "I didn't know you had come inside. You scared the living daylights out of me."

"And *you* skeered the livin' daylights outta *me*!" he exclaimed, plopping down on the moss-covered ground inside the thicket. "I just wanted to come in and rest for a minute."

"Only for a *little* minute," I said. "Mama might be upset if she finds out we came out here this late."

"Yeah, especially since she told us about the hobos she saw in the neighborhood today."

"As much as we have those homeless hobos coming in off the tracks around here, you'd think she wouldn't pay much attention to it."

"I know. It seems like havin' hobos around is a fact of life when you live near the railroad. As Papa says," and here Edward dropped his voice to sound more like a man, "'Call them hobos or bums or tramps, it don't really matter, but one thing's for sure. Most of them are out of a home, and they're down on their luck. We jest need t' help 'em out, as best we can.'"

"You sound so much like Papa when you talk that way," I smiled, "but we'd better get going. It's getting darker out there by the minute."

Just then, there was a loud snapping sound nearby. "What was that?" I whispered.

"Shhh," Ed responded with his finger to his lips. "Listen."

Chill bumps popped out on my arms again.

There was another snap . . . and another . . . and still another. Something alive was rustling through the leaves toward us here in the middle of the darkening woods. Something big!

We sat like statues inside the hideout as the sounds came closer. Only our eyes shifted to look at each other. I could distinctly make out the sound of feet shuffling through the leaves, but there was more. It was a puffing kind of sound, like someone out of breath. There was a squeaking sound, too. Then we heard voices, soft and low at first, but gradually getting louder.

We crept to the inside edge of our hiding place so that we might peek out without being seen. In the gathering twilight, I could make out the forms of two men. One of them was pushing a wheelbarrow. To my great alarm, the men stopped right outside our hideout.

The first man had long red hair with a bushy red beard that matched. He was carrying a shovel.

The second one had a round belly that stuck out over the top of his pants. His clothes looked dirty and ragged; his face, covered with stubby whiskers. A greasy-looking felt hat perched on his head while an unlit stub of a cigar dangled from the corner of his mouth. He was breathing hard from pushing the wheelbarrow.

I peered through my uneven peephole, wondering if these men were the ones who had scared Mama earlier in the day. My heart pounded inside my chest. It was so loud, I was afraid they might hear it!

The hobo with the stubby whiskers struck a match to light his cigar. The flare from the flame allowed me to see the wheelbarrow more clearly. It was old and rickety-looking. A large mound covered with burlap bags totally filled it. Dark red stains on the bags seemed to glare at me.

I glanced at Edward with enormous eyes. I wanted to scream, I was so scared.

The men began to speak again. One of them rolled his rrrr's around on his tongue when he spoke. "Herre by these bushes looks like a good spot to burry 'im," he said. "It's out o' the way, so nobody's likely t' spot 'im herre."

"If you think it's fur enough away from the railroad tracks, then I reckon it'll be okay," the other man drawled in a deep, raspy voice.

"All rrright then. I'll start the diggin'. You brring the wheelbarrow on 'round."

"Will do, Scottie, but ye'd best dig as fast as ye can. We need to git the buryin' done before it gits completely dark," replied the raspy voice.

"Aye," the red-bearded man answered. He used the point of his shovel to tap into the soil before he began to dig.

As I turned to look at my brother, I saw fear in his eyes. Not only were these tramps trespassing in our family's woods, but they were digging a hole and were planning to *bury* something! Or *somebody*!

After he had plunked some shovels full of dirt into a pile, the man with the red beard paused from his digging. He leaned on the shovel and looked around while he wiped his forehead with a dirty handkerchief. "Nobody'll everr think to look for 'im away out herre." He stuffed the handkerchief into his pocket and went back to work.

"I hope not," agreed his partner. "I feel sorry for any poor sucker that happens onto this buryin' spot. We're a'goin' to bury him deep, so's people will never know what happened to 'im. Here, now, let me take a turn at the diggin'." He moved so that he could take the shovel.

Edward and I squeezed each other's hands. I was terrified.

As the digging continued and the mound of dirt grew bigger, Edward started backing away from his peephole. I did the same. We had to be careful not to make a sound. Silently, we crept across the mossy floor toward the small open space on the other side. With the crown in my hand, I followed Edward out of the hideout.

We knew we had to move with caution. One stir of the dried leaves covering the path could call attention to our presence. We crawled on our hands and knees, moving slowly, slowly, ever-so-slowly.

I felt a sharp stab of pain in the palm of my hand. It hurt so much I wanted to holler, but I bit my lips together instead. I looked to see what had caused the pain. It was a prickly ball from a sweet gum tree. It had made tiny dents in my palm. Quietly, I tossed it beside the trail and rubbed my hand.

I began moving again. A twig cracked beneath my knee. The sound was so loud, it sounded like a rifle shot! Both of us froze, afraid they might have heard and would come after us. We waited for what seemed forever. Finally, Edward began to move again. I followed, looking carefully at the trail. Another broken stick might bring disaster!

As we crept along, an owl suddenly swooped down just above our heads. Edward gasped loudly, then clapped his hand over his mouth to stifle a yell. Once again we stayed frozen until we were sure his sound had not been heard.

Finally, we were safely out of hearing range. We stood up and ran along the leaf-covered path toward home as fast as our bare feet could run. We raced across the wet, muddy area of the marshy bog, and slid down the steep incline. We only slowed a little as we came to the edge of the railroad tracks. Quickly, we jumped over them.

At last we were on the house-side of the tracks. We plopped down beside a bunch of red sumac and golden-orange sassafras bushes to catch our breath. We peered over the leafy limbs and listened. There was definitely a thumping sound. Was it footsteps pounding down the pathway we had just traveled? Were the hobos hot on our trail? We gripped each other's hands, waiting. Waiting . . . watching . . . listening . . .

CHAPTER 2

"Do you hear it, Ed? Is it them? Are they coming after us?" I panted breathlessly.

"Don't know," he whispered back.

We didn't blink an eye as we watched the trail across the tracks. Nobody appeared. Gradually the sound grew quieter. Then Edward laughed. "It was just our own heartbeats thumping," he said sheepishly.

"Whew," I sighed in relief, putting my hand over my heart. "But what was going on back there?"

"All I know is . . . those two men are up to no good," he answered in a worried voice.

"Did you recognize them?"

"Sure, didn't you?"

"Right away," I answered. "One was Smokey Joe. He's the man who rescued Maggie from the railroad tracks one day when she was a kitten."

"I remember that. And the man with the accent was Scottie. He's the one who sorted and juggled potatoes in our backyard last summer. Mama always fixes them some food when they do things to help her. I had the feelin' both of them was nice."

"If they're that nice, why did Mama bother to tell us about them being back in the neighborhood?" I asked.

"And what were they doin' back there? They were talkin' about buryin' something big! What are they mixed up with?" Edward asked. "And what can we do about it?"

Just then we heard Mama calling. "Emma Mae? Edward? Where *are* you two?" There was a pause while she waited for an answer. Neither of us moved. "Are you finished with your chores? You're not goin' to that party tonight unless your chores are done!" she yelled.

For some reason, we remained quiet. We heard the screen door slam shut.

"Are we going to tell Mama and Papa what we saw?" I asked.

We sat there in the twilight thinking about that for a minute. The full moon rising above our barn looked like a huge orange pumpkin floating in the sky. The tall dead oak tree beside the corncrib was a silhouette against the moon. It looked spooky, foreboding. We heard the evening chorus of croaking tree frogs and katydids as we sat in silence, thinking about what to do.

The feeling that something strange was about to happen came over me again, causing the hairs on my arms to stand out once more.

Edward said, "Why don't we wait 'til tomorrow—*after* the party?"

"Emma Mae? Edward?" Mama's call echoed through the deepening darkness, followed by the familiar slamming of the door.

I looked back across the tracks and saw the evening star in the west. It seemed to be winking at me, like it was keeping a secret.

"I agree, Ed. Let's wait." I winked back at the star. "This is our first time to be invited to the big party. We've just *got* to go. If we tell them now, they might make us stay home tonight. We'll just wait and tell them tomorrow." I jumped to my feet. "Come on! Beat you to the house!"

And, with that, I picked up the paper crown and took off at a run with Edward by my side. Our bare feet sailed back down the hard dirt path, past the sweet potato cellar, and through the garden gate.

We could smell supper cooking as we ran up the back steps and into the kitchen. The door banged shut behind us. Mama looked up when we rushed in. She was stirring fried potatoes. I could smell turnip greens cooking. "There you are," she said crossly. "I was beginning to think some goblins had come along and gobbled you up. What have you two been up to?"

"We finished our chores and took a quick run to our hideout to get my crown," I explained, glancing at Edward as he walked through the kitchen to the sitting room. I placed the golden paper crown on my head. "See? How do you like it?"

Mama looked at me in my crown and smiled a small smile, but she said in her fussy voice, "You know I don't like you runnin' off to the woods like that when it's this late."

"But we made it back just fine, Mama." I washed my hands in the wash pan on a small table near the door and dried them on the drying rag that hung on a nail next to it. "Now, what can I do to help?"

"I was needin' you to cook the cornbread fritters."

She had already made the batter. All I had to do was drop little scoops of it onto the hot grease in the big iron skillet, making nice, round circles. When bubbles started to show on the tops of the fritters, I flipped them over until they were crusty brown on both sides. Then I poured fresh buttermilk into the glasses on the table.

The entire time I was working, I talked. I told Mama about things that had happened at school today. I told her about feeding the chickens and about how many eggs I had gathered from the henhouse. I even told her about the big pumpkin moon rising above the barn. But what I *didn't* tell her was about our fright in the woods.

Mama's fretful look had faded now. She actually smiled as she said, "Before we call the others to eat, let me fetch my surprise." She disappeared through the curtains that covered the door to the pantry, then came back out, carrying a pumpkin with a carved face.

"Oh, Mama!" I exclaimed. "It's so scary! It's perfect for tonight." I jumped up and down in excitement. My crown nearly fell off my head.

She went to the wood-burning cook stove and removed one of the covers. Carefully, she picked up a small, flaming stick of wood that she used to light the candle inside the Jack-o-Lantern. I put the glowing pumpkin in the middle of the table.

"Since you're the queen tonight, Emma Mae, why don't you sit at the head of the table? You can call the family to eat now."

I went to the doorway and called out, "My loyal subjects. You may now come and join Her Highness for dinner." I stood with my head held high, looking down my nose, as Papa and all my brothers came trooping into the kitchen. Each of them bowed to me when they entered the room, except for Baby Arthur, of course. Papa was carrying the baby in his arms. With the gleaming pumpkin on the table and the queen giving commands, the simple meal became a party.

After supper, I put my crown aside and helped Mama clean up the kitchen. I carried the supper scraps and dishwater to the slop bucket that had been returned to its spot beside the back door. This slop would go out to the hogs for tomorrow night's feeding. I finished sweeping the floor and covered the butter dish and other items on the table with a clean tablecloth.

At last the moment had arrived for me to ask my long-anticipated question. I cleared my throat and, in a small voice, I said, *Mutter?* That's the German word for Mother. I sometimes called her that, especially when I wanted something in a big way. *"Mutter,* can you please get the dress I've asked about wearing as part of my queen's costume?"

I held my breath, waiting for her response. I was so afraid she would say 'no,' I could hardly breathe. She stood there, looking at me. I clasped my hands in front of me in a pleading way, jiggling them slightly. I smiled my most persuasive smile. "Please?"

To my great relief, she smiled back! She turned and went to her bedroom closet.

The dress I had dreamed about wearing was a long blue velvet dress with a white lace collar and shiny buttons down the front. It had belonged to my great-grandmother, Mary Katherine, who had died long before I was born. I knew the precious dress had come from

Germany when our ancestors arrived in America on a ship in 1845, more than sixty-nine years ago.

According to the stories told about her, Mary Katherine had worn the dress when she told fairy tales to children. It was also said that she usually wore a crown to make her look like a fairy queen. That's why I had made the crown—hoping that I would be able to wear the dress to the party tonight.

I waited in the middle of the kitchen floor with my fingers crossed behind my back for good luck. It seemed like forever before she returned, but she was carrying the dress across her arm!

"It's goin' to be mighty big around your middle, Emma Mae," she said, "but you're tall for your age, so I reckon you're tall enough to wear it. Try it on, so we can see how it looks."

I rushed into my little bedroom and took off my work clothes. I held my arms over my head while Mama slipped the dress on me. She was right. It was much too big around the middle until she tightened the ribbon belt, but the length was perfect.

"Oh, I just *love* it!" I cried, jumping up and down again. "*Danke*, Mama!" I peered into the little mirror that hung beside the washstand in my room. In the reflection, I could see my slender face with the dark brown eyes sparkling with excitement. The brown hair hanging loosely around my shoulders, though, was not right.

"I've got to do something about my hair," I said. "It definitely doesn't look like a queen's hairdo." I plaited it into one long braid and coiled it on top of my head, pinning it in place with hairpins. I put the paper crown around it, so that it encircled my head. It was perfect.

Mama nodded her approval just as Edward walked into the room.

"Well, here comes our ship's captain," she said. "Don't you look fancy?"

Ed was wearing an old white shirt that he had tucked into some tight-fitting black knickers. He had a flat white cap with a black bill perched jauntily on his head, and a rubber dagger stuck into the waistline of his pants.

"Mama, do I look more like the captain of a ship from the 1840's . . . or a pirate?" he asked.

"Well, maybe a little of both," Mama laughed, "but you look just fine. You both look just fine."

She turned abruptly and walked out of my room. She was only gone a minute before she came back with a little container in her hands. "You need a little paint on your cheeks if you're goin' to be a queen, Emma Mae," she said as she dipped the tip of her finger into the little pot of rouge. She smeared it on my cheeks in large pink circles. She also put a little of the color on my lips.

"While I'm at it, Edward, I think the sea captain could use a little color as part of his costume, too." She rubbed small blushes of the paint on Edward's cheeks.

"Now you're both ready." She stood back to look us over. Still smiling, she went to the door and called out, "Papa! You and the boys need to come take a look at our Halloween spooks!"

Papa came into the room carrying Baby Arthur. Four-year old William and seven-year old Frederick trailed along behind him.

Mama said, "Our little *Fraulein* is growin' up." This was another German word that sometimes slipped into our conversation. I knew that *Fraulein* meant "young lady."

"And so is our *Junger Mann*," she added. In German that meant "young man."

I curtsied to Papa, and Edward bowed. "You both look mighty nice," he said, "but, Emma Mae, you be careful wearin' that dress. It's a family treasure, and don't you forget it!"

"I won't forget, Papa. I'll be ever-so-careful in it."

"Now all we need is Clarence. Where *is* that boy?" he asked. "I haven't seen him since supper."

The words had barely left Papa's lips when there was a loud knock at the back door. It was more of a pounding sound than a knock. Bam! Bam! Bam!

My heart sank in my chest. All evening, in the back of my mind, I had worried about the two men in the woods. Could that be who was pounding on the door? Edward and I grabbed each other's hands in fear.

Mama hurried across the kitchen. The only light was from the low-lit coal oil lamp and the Jack-o-Lantern glowing on the table. We followed her. As she opened the door, someone yelled and reached in to try and grab Mama. She jumped backwards, but the person charged in after her—right into the middle of our kitchen! Mama and I both screamed!

The intruder was a hobo, all right, but I could tell at a glance he was *not* one of the men we had seen earlier in the evening. This one wore a loose-fitting shirt with ragged pants held up by suspenders. He wore big shoes on his feet and a floppy hat on his head. His face was dirty and smudged. A red bandanna bundle was tied to the end of a long stick that he held over his shoulder.

Both Baby Arthur and Little Will started to cry. Seven-year-old Frederick jumped behind Papa, peering around in fright.

Jiggs, our little three-legged black-and-white terrier, who had lost a hind leg in a train accident, began to bark, yipping at the legs of the intruder. When he got excited like this, he could actually balance on his one back leg with his front legs held up in front of him. It was quite an accomplishment for a three-legged dog.

The hobo looked around at all of us. By this time, everybody was standing perfectly still, staring in fright at this strange-looking person in the middle of our kitchen. Everybody, that is, except Jiggs, who kept barking and yipping at the stranger, hopping up and down on his one hind leg.

All of a sudden, the hobo began to laugh—softly at first, but gradually louder. As he laughed, he began to dance. He used the hobo stick like a walking cane as he did a tap dance routine known as the soft-shoe shuffle.

While he laughed and danced, we began to laugh, too, because we recognized the sound of that laughter as well as the dance steps.

It was only Clarence, dressed up in his Halloween costume, ready to go to the party!

"You gave us quite a scare, young man," Mama fussed, playfully shaking his shoulders.

Jiggs kept barking. We told him to hush, but he just hobbled around. Part of the time he was down on all three legs; then he would balance on one leg again.

"That'll do, boy," Edward finally said to the little dog. Immediately on hearing this command, he quit his barking and sat down on his haunches.

Papa got the coal oil lantern down off the nail by the back door. He lifted the lantern's glass globe while Clarence struck a match to light the wick. When the flame grew tall, he turned the little knob to adjust the flame to just the right size. Carefully, he slipped the glass globe back down into place. That would keep the flame from being blown out by the wind.

"How long will it take us to walk to Krebs Station, Clarence?" I asked.

Clarence was fourteen years old and had been to the Halloween parties at the train station before. That's why our parents had asked him to escort us tonight.

"It won't take all that long," he replied, "if we don't meet up with any unexpected spooks along the way." He laughed as he made this remark, but Edward and I exchanged worried glances. We were nervous about walking the tracks, even in the opposite direction from our earlier scare.

Clarence went to the back door, swinging the lantern in one hand and propping the long stick over his shoulder with the other. "You still want to go, youngsters?" he asked with a smirk in his voice. "It's time to go . . . *if you dare!*"

I squeezed my feet into my Sunday shoes and buttoned them up. Somehow it didn't seem right for a fairy queen to be barefooted. "Of course, I want to go, you knave," I answered my older brother. "And since I'm the queen, I not only *want* to go, I *demand* to go!" I hoped that my voice sounded confident, because, inside, I felt as nervous as Edward looked. Who knew what would be waiting for us when we got to the railroad tracks!!

CHAPTER 3

Clarence opened the back screen door and stepped outside, rudely letting it slam shut behind him. Edward and I followed him out, with Mama following us. She carried the glowing Jack-o-Lantern and placed it on the top step. Its deliciously scary face lit up the darkness. Maggie, my black cat, sat down beside the pumpkin, switching her tail back and forth, back and forth. As I turned to wave goodbye to Mama, I saw a perfect Halloween scene.

We walked on the dusty path that led around the house to the little stretch of gravel road in front of our place. This road led up the slight rise to the railroad tracks. The flickering beam from the lantern lit the way.

It wasn't until we got to the tracks that we noticed Jiggs, trotting along behind us. "Go back home, you dumb dog," Clarence ordered curtly, but the dog kept coming, wagging his short, stubby tail.

Clarence turned left onto the tracks in the direction of the party. I reached over and grabbed Edward's hand. Both of us stopped dead still, peering anxiously into the darkness in the opposite direction, back toward the woods. At that moment, the full moon popped out from behind a cloud, lighting the world around us. We stood like statues, staring down the tracks in the direction of the scene of the crime. Seeing nothing stirring, we turned away from it and quickly covered the distance to catch up with our big brother, who was walking on ahead.

In his usual annoying manner, Clarence said, "What's wrong with you two? Got the heebie-jeebies?" He laughed loudly, then picked up a rock from the side of the tracks and threw it at Jiggs. The little dog just kept on trotting along behind us.

"You can't go to the party, you half-witted critter. It's not the kind of party a dog would like. Git on back home now. Git!" He threw another rock in Jiggs' direction.

"How do you know?" I asked Clarence as I began to adjust my steps to the space between the crossties of the railroad tracks.

"How do I know what?" Now Clarence was growling at *me*.

"How do you know it's not the kind of party a dog would like?" I said, persisting.

"Because it's a people party, for cryin' out loud. Dogs aren't invited to *people* parties!" As Clarence said those words, he leaned over, picked up some more small rocks, and threw them in the direction of the little dog that was hobbling along with his funny, three-legged gait.

Jiggs continued to ignore Clarence's loud commands and rocks as he kept jumping from crosstie to crosstie. He seemed determined to go to the party with us. "Why don't you just leave him alone?" Edward asked. "He won't bother anybody. You know what a good little fellow he is."

"Well," Clarence grumbled, "I don't want to spend time taking him back, so I guess he'll just have to go with us. But I won't be responsible for him!" he added, making his point.

By this time we had walked a short distance down the tracks and were crossing over the trestle. I always felt uneasy walking across this train bridge. There were no handrails on a trestle that could prevent a person from falling over the side into the depths below.

We walked in silence for a few steps before Clarence muttered, "Stupid mutt! Whoever heard of a stupid mutt tagging along to a Halloween party?"

I couldn't help smiling, thinking how Clarence must feel to have three tagalongs. I wondered if he felt as embarrassed at having a younger sister and brother trailing behind him as he did a pet dog, but I didn't ask.

The moon seemed to be playing a game of "Now You See Me, Now You Don't," as it darted in and out around the fast-moving clouds. The air felt hot and humid. Usually at Halloween the weather is cool; sometimes even cold . . . but not this year. Everywhere I went, people talked about the unseasonable weather we were having.

As we walked along at a brisk pace, I began to sweat in the heavy velvet dress. My shoes hurt my feet. The wind blew in strong gusts, swirling up little whirlwinds of dried grass and debris along the sides of the tracks—like fairy twirls in the moonlight.

Then we heard a different sound. It was dim at first but, gradually, as we scurried along, it became louder. It was the sound of music blending with the sounds of the night. "Listen!" I said excitely. "I hear music!"

"Well, hurray for Emma Mae," Clarence said sarcastically. "She passed the hearing test!"

I knew he was trying to get me upset by saying that, but tonight, with my special costume on, with the Hide-and-Go-Seek moon dancing overhead, and with fiddle music in the distance, I didn't let it bother me. After all, I was the queen!

As the sounds of music grew louder, I also felt my excitement grow. When the memory of the experience earlier in the woods flashed through my mind, I pushed it aside. Just now, it all seemed far away.

Jiggs had begun to fall behind because of the fast pace Clarence was setting with his long legs. Edward picked his dog up and carried him. "Hey, Jiggs," Edward said as he ruffled up the little dog's hair on top of his head. "Can you hear that harmonica playing with the fiddle?"

Edward had a harmonica of his own that he always carried in his pocket. He often played it when we were in our hideout or around the house at night. He could play just about any tune on his little instrument. Papa said Edward had a natural ear for music.

I reached over and patted his arm. We exchanged smiles. "What a night this is going to be," I whispered.

"What a night!" Edward agreed.

If we had only known . . . . . !

CHAPTER 4

We had walked to Krebs Station many times in the daylight. Besides being a small railroad station for local passengers, we knew there was a switch track there. Every day the engineers switched train cars from one track to another by means of a system of levers. We had been there before when freight trains were switched off the main track in order to allow the faster-moving passenger trains to pass through. Only local trains stopped at Krebs Station.

On my visits there, I had seen the semicircle of neat cottages behind the small train station. Employees of the railroad company lived in these little houses. Some of them had families with children who came to our one-room school named Sunny Slope School, which was located not far away. In front of the semicircle of houses was a common space that looked like a park, with shade trees and a neatly mown lawn.

One large house stood next to this complex. It belonged to the Dexter family. Mr. Dexter was the stationmaster, the main person in charge of the station and the switch tracks. Anybody could tell just by looking at the house from the outside that the Dexter family was wealthy. This meant that they were a bit different from most of the people who lived in the neighborhood. For example, the yard at the Dexter Place had a white picket fence around it. The house was always freshly painted, and there were lace curtains in all the windows. Even the porch furniture wore a coat of paint. Also, the lower part of the tree trunks in their yard gleamed with whitewash, a white painting solution sometimes painted on trees. Only rich people had whitewashed trees.

But even though we were familiar with the outdoor setting around Krebs Station, we were surprised when we walked into the circle of light at the Halloween party. Ghosts made from sheets and pillowcases billowed in the gusty wind as if they were alive. Glowing lanterns hung from all the trees. Torches and Jack-o-Lanterns gleamed. In the center of the circle, a bonfire cast its flickering shadows in all directions.

A platform had been built for the musicians. Three men and two women sat in a semicircle on this little stage. The main performer was a fiddler. A guitarist provided backup music, along with a man playing a homemade bass fiddle.

The big bass fiddle had been made from an upside-down washtub. A hoe handle was sticking up from a hole in the middle of the tub. A thin rope was attached at an angle, so that it could be plucked, adding background beats to the music.

"Look over yonder," I said to Edward, pointing at one of the women in the group. "She's playing the spoons like we do at home." The older woman was holding two large metal spoons so that they clicked down over the outstretched fingers on her other hand. She was keeping up the rhythm of the band. Occasionally, she made rhythmic sounds by scraping a hard object up and down over the ridges of a metal washboard—the kind like Mama used to scrub our clothes on washday.

The other woman was the harmonica player. While she played well, she was not as good as Edward, I thought proudly.

Everybody at the party was wearing a costume. I saw my cousin Pearl, who was also my best friend, waving at me. "Emma Mae," she called. "Come on over. I saved you a seat." Pearl, dressed up in a fat lady costume, had pillows stuffed inside her dress to make her look big. I hurried over to sit with her.

Our seats were near the bonfire. We listened to the music, sometimes clapping our hands or singing along. During one of the songs, a few of the older kids got up and started to dance. Clarence was the best one there, doing his soft-shoe shuffle routine with his hobo stick like he had done in our kitchen earlier. When the other dancers saw how well he danced, they stepped back and let him dance alone.

But what made it even better was Jiggs! When Jiggs saw Clarence doing his fancy dancing, he jumped out of Edward's lap and started to bark. Then he did his barking and balancing act, jumping around on his one hind leg. He hopped around and around Clarence as he danced to the lively music.

The crowd started laughing and cheering. Edward stood at the side of the area and clapped his hands in rhythm to the music. It seemed like the more he clapped, the more Jiggs barked and jumped around. To make it even better, Edward got his harmonica out of his pocket and joined in the music. They were very good, I thought, even if they *were* my family. It was a truly delightful act!

When the music ended, Clarence made deep bows, swooping his floppy hat in front of him in one hand while holding his hobo stick in the other. Jiggs quit barking as soon as the music stopped. Now Edward bent down and picked him up. He held the little dog so he could move his pet's head and front paws in a bowing manner. Finally, Edward took a bow. The crowd cheered and cheered.

"Come on, Emma Mae," Pearl said. "Let's go bob for apples. Maybe that will cool me off." She was sweating in her costume on this hot, humid night.

We walked over to get in line. The people in front of us took turns dunking their heads into a tub of water filled with floating apples. Each person pushed an apple to the bottom of the tub where they would try to sink their teeth into it. If they succeeded, they would pull the apple out of the water and eat it.

"You go ahead, Pearl," I teased as she knelt down to take her turn, "but that is much below the dignity of the queen." I stood aside with my head held high, looking down my nose at the apple-bobbers.

After that, there were other games to play. We threw darts at targets painted on pumpkins, ate marshmallows that were dangling from strings, and tried guessing how many kernels of shelled corn were in a fruit jar. We ate our fill of homemade cookies and gingerbread, and then washed it all down with fresh apple cider drawn from the spigot of a big wooden barrel.

I noticed that Jiggs was being fed cookies by almost everybody, as he hobbled around the circle. He seemed to be enjoying the merry gathering as much as anybody there. Ha, ha, Clarence, I thought to myself. He does like people parties, after all.

Now that our bellies were full and the games had ended, we heard Mr. Dexter, the stationmaster, call out. "Gather 'round, you goblins and gremlins. The time has come to tell our tales."

As we came together in a close circle around the bonfire, I had a slight shiver. I knew the scary part of the evening was about to begin. Most of the torches had been extinguished so the only light was from the low-burning bonfire and a few of the flickering Jack-o-Lanterns. Occasionally, the full moon peeped out from behind a dark cloud, but it seemed to be staying away more, now that the clouds were getting larger.

When the ghost stories began, Pearl and I sat as close together as we could get. One person told stories of strange happenings in graveyards. Another told of appearances of people who had died long ago. Still another person described a house that was haunted by pale, shadowy apparitions.

Then Mr. Dexter stood up again. Suddenly we forgot that he was the stationmaster and the father of a few of our friends. He became a master storyteller.

"My story is about a man who liked to go out in the swamps on hot, sultry nights to talk with the will-o'-the wisp," he began.

I knew that a will-o'-the-wisp was a shifting, moving flame that could sometimes be seen over marshy areas at night. I had also learned in school that this kind of light occurred only when certain weather conditions were present, like when hot, moist air mixes suddenly with colder air. This was the very kind of weather we were having tonight.

Mr. Dexter continued. "This 'willer-de-wisp' was not just a light, though. This one could actually come alive, at times, and make itself present to people if they happened to be searching for it. The man in my story was one of those.

"He lived in these hereabout parts. Your grandpappy or your grandmammy might have knowed who he was. He would sneak out of his house late at night, while his family was asleep. If he saw a 'willer-de-wisp,' he would follow that flickering light all around the countryside. Sometimes he would do deeds of meanness, like opening barn lot gates so cattle could get out, or stealing chickens and eggs . . . *if* the light told him to. It has even been told that, with the light urging him on, he pushed wagons into ponds and put porch furniture up on rooftops. But always after he had committed his deeds of mischief, he would say . . ." and here Mr. Dexter raised his voice to a high, mournful sound, "'The 'willer-de-wisp' tole me to. The 'willer-de-wisp' tole me to.'"

The way he said those words was terrifying. "So beware, all of you within the sound of my voice," he continued in his scary-sounding tone. "Beware the 'willer-de-wisp,' for it can trap anybody. It can even . . . trap . . . YOU!"

He lurched out at his audience when he said that word. We all jumped and squealed, like he knew we would. He continued in his quavery voice. "And when it traps you, no matter who you are, it can lead you astray. It might have you do things you never thought you would do. And all you will be able to say is, 'The "willer-de-wisp" tole me to. The "willer-de-wisp" tole me to . . . tole me to . . . tole me to . . .'"

His haunting voice trailed off into silence. He bowed to his audience, which indicated that his story had ended. We applauded him loudly for his scary tale.

As people settled back in their spaces, another person walked over to the platform and stood beside the low-burning fire. It was a man

I had never seen before. He was very distinguished looking, dressed in a brown business suit and vest. He wore a white shirt with a bow tie. A black derby hat sat perched on his head. With his dark, intense eyes, he was quite impressive.

"Who's that?" I asked Pearl. She made a funny face and shrugged her shoulders. I could see puzzled looks on the faces of people all around the circle, as they asked each other the same question. Each time the response was a shaking of heads and a baffled look. Apparently, nobody knew this storyteller. It was as though he had just magically appeared.

"My story tonight is about a mystery train," he began. He spoke in a deep, secretive-sounding voice with a strange kind of accent. "It's also about *me*—the night I was captured by that evil train."

People began to squirm uneasily—partly from what he was saying and partly because of the way he looked each of us in the eye. Those dark, sharp eyes didn't miss a person. Even little Jiggs, sitting beside Edward near the front of the circle, was as still as a statue.

"You see," continued the stranger, "I was out walking along the railroad tracks late one evening, on my way to keep an appointment. It was a hot, humid night—much like this very night, as I recall. There was a brisk breeze blowing and a full moon that ducked in and out from behind fast-moving clouds." He gestured to the sky with his hands. At the very moment he said this, a big cloud blotted out the moon.

"But as I walked, I had this peculiar feeling that something was about to happen. I turned in the darkness and looked up the tracks in the opposite direction. And that's when I first saw the strange light approaching.

"At first I thought it was the will-o'-the-wisp, which I had often seen before, but this light was different. It kept moving toward me. Faster and faster did it come. I knew it was not a regular train, because there was no sound. Just the light! I tried to run, but it seemed as if my feet were frozen to the ground. I tried to dodge the light, but I couldn't budge.

"Not a sound did it make in the darkness, this mysterious light in the night. Not a sound did I hear in the darkness, but brighter it grew. So bright!

"It swept down the tracks right at me. The light was brighter than day. I knew when it hit I'd be done for! There was no way to escape! No way!"

The stranger's voice rose even louder, yet there was still a note of secrecy, as if he were letting us in on some kind of plot.

"Not until it was almost upon me did I realize that the light actually *was* attached to something. What was it? Why, it was a train—a soundless, nearly invisible train—swooping me off in the darkness, swooping me off in the night, swooping me off forever, never again to see light."

I was spellbound, motionless. I could not take my eyes off the storyteller's face as he said the refrain over and over again. His dark eyes, now large and haunting, moved from face to face around the still crowd. They had taken on a frightening, frantic look. He opened them still wider, arching his eyebrows; looking at each of us.

"So beware of the mystery train, for it may come looking for you. And when it does it can swoop *you* off in the darkness, swoop *you* off in the night, swoop *you* off forever . . . never again to see light!"

The voice gradually grew softer until it was just a loud whisper of ". . . never again to see light." The storyteller, now silent, stood frozen in place. And we sat there. Not a movement could be seen; not a sound could be heard except the moaning of the wind in the trees overhead. It was as though we had all been hypnotized.

Finally, something moved. It was Jiggs. He jumped up on all three legs, bared his teeth at the stranger, and growled. Then he started barking at the man in the brown suit. It was not the same kind of barking he had done before. This time it was a mean-sounding, ferocious kind of bark with growling deep in his throat.

That was all it took to bring everybody out of the spell the stranger had created with his story. We looked around for him, but he had vanished.

Pearl and I had been gripping each other's hands during the entire story. Now we unlaced our hands and I hugged her goodbye, squeezing the fat pillows of her costume as I reached around her. "See you later," we whispered.

All around the circle, people talked quietly about the man and his mysterious story. We got together with our own families or friends as we began to leave, waving at each other, calling our goodbyes.

This last story had somehow put a subdued ending to an otherwise wonderful party—one that no one there would ever forget. Especially the three of us. And Jiggs.

CHAPTER 5

On the walk home, we trudged silently along the railroad tracks. The only sounds were those of the nighttime insects and creatures in the surrounding darkness. Edward carried Jiggs. He acted like he didn't feel well. Too many cookies, we figured.

Clarence, carrying the lantern again, walked more slowly now. He seemed to want to stay close to us, even if we *were* his little sister and brother. I suddenly felt an urge to confide in him about the frightening experience that Edward and I had shared in the woods earlier in the evening.

"Clarence," I said.

He jumped, startled, as my voice broke the silence. "What is it, Emma Mae?"

"I was just wondering about something. Could Ed and I share a secret with you?" I looked around at Edward. I could see his look of approval even in the near-darkness.

"Sure, if you want to. What?" Clarence asked.

"Well, you see . . . ," I hardly knew where to start. But once I began, the story tumbled out. Edward helped me explain the entire incident of seeing the hobos in the woods.

"That's wild!" Clarence exclaimed. "Do you think you could take me to the spot and let me see the grave for myself?"

"Now? Tonight?" Edward cried out. "There is no way you're getting me out in those woods tonight!"

"Oh, come on, you two. It wouldn't take but a minute, if you're telling the truth," Clarence persisted.

"We'll take you there tomorrow, Clarence, but, please, not tonight," I begged. "We probably shouldn't have told you."

"Well, I don't believe you anyway," he said in his sarcastic way. "You're just making it up. It never even happened."

"It happened all right," answered Edward, "and we can prove it. Can't we, Emma Mae?"

"Sure," I said, "but in the daylight. I am not *about* to go in there tonight!"

By this time we were standing in the middle of the railroad crossing on the gravel road that led down the little hill to our house. We were nearly home. But Clarence, who was holding the lantern, just stood there between the tracks, teasing us.

"You're just a couple of scaredy-cats," he said. "There's nothing that can hurt you in these woods. Come on. Show me that *grave* you saw those men digging, *if* you saw anything at all."

"Oh, come on, Emma Mae, let's go show him," Edward said. "It won't take a minute."

"No!" I said emphatically. "I'm too tired, and my feet hurt. Besides, I'm sure Mama and Papa are wondering where we are."

Now Clarence and Edward were both in the mood to see the grave. They teased me and begged me until, even though I knew we shouldn't go that late at night, I reluctantly gave in. The gooseflesh on my arms was constant now. I felt like I was inside of a bad dream..

I turned and started moving down the tracks again, walking slowly, slowly, slowly over the short distance, until we came to the path that led from the railroad tracks to the marshy bog. We went up the embankment and into the edge of the darkness.

It was totally black in the woods. The moon had long since vanished behind dark clouds. I stopped for a minute, aware of the heavy velvet dress hanging on my body. And, of my aching feet! The wind was blowing much stronger now, moaning and sighing through the trees. I shivered. The temperature was dropping fast.

"The weather conditions are just right for the will-o'-the-wisp to show up," I whispered to my brothers in a quavery voice, hoping to scare them into changing their minds. The three of us stood completely still, absorbing the blackness just beyond the lantern light. Jiggs continued to sleep in Edward's arms.

"Do you still want to go look for a grave?" I asked softly.

In answer, Clarence held the kerosene lamp out to me. "You lead the way," he said.

With a heavy sigh, I took the lantern and led my brothers over the leaf-covered maze of trails I knew so well. It wasn't long until we came to the group of bushes that was our hideout. I stopped outside the small opening that formed our entrance.

"Since we're here," I said quietly, "I might as well get my doll and take her home for the night, in case it rains." I disappeared through the gap in the hedge. Clarence poked his head inside.

"So this is where you two hang out all the time," he whispered. "I'll have to admit it's a great hideout." He backed away from the bushes as I crawled out with the lantern in my hand and Maizey under my arm.

Clarence resumed his teasing. "But where's the *grave* you were talking about?"

"It's around this way," Edward muttered, stifling a yawn. He sounded tired. He took the lantern from me and led the way around the thicket to the other side, and there it was. The large mound of fresh dirt seemed to gleam in the dim light. It was the grave.

Clarence's eyes looked huge in the lamplight. "Why, you weren't teasing me, after all," he said in a whisper. "It really *is* a grave." He leaned over and picked up a stick. "Here," he said, "let's dig a little and see what's in there." Edward set the lantern down, while Clarence began to scratch into the soft dirt piled in the middle of the mound.

"Wait a minute," I whispered. "What's that smell?" Clarence stopped his digging and sniffed. "I smell smoke!" I whispered more loudly. "Something's burning!"

"I smell it, too!" Edward exclaimed.

Frantically, we looked around. Not far away, through the growth of tall trees and bushes, we could see a campfire. Its orange flames flared into the darkness. Shadowy figures moved around it. We froze with fear when we realized it was more than just a campfire. There was also a torch! And the torch had begun to move . . . in our direction!

We stood in stunned disbelief. Illuminated in the light from the torch were two angry faces. One of the faces had a bushy red beard and the other one had stubby whiskers. Without a doubt, it was the same hobos who had dug the grave . . . and they were moving in our direction, fast!

"Let's get out of here!" Now it was Clarence shouting the command. He grabbed the lantern and started to run, but, not being familiar with the area, he ran the wrong way.

"This way, Clarence," I cried. "Hurry! It's this way back to the tracks!"

Clarence's miscue had given the hobos an advantage. Jiggs was awake now and barking his head off. It was all Edward could do to hold onto him as we dashed through the bushes and trees, heading toward the railroad tracks.

Clarence, still holding the wildly swinging lantern, took off down another wrong path. As I reached to grab him, I dropped Maizey. "Clarence!" I called. "Not that way! Here! Hold the light still so I can get my doll!" He whirled around so I could see. I grabbed the doll with one hand and clutched his arm with the other. "Let me lead the way," I said.

But the delays were taking too much time. Our pursuers were gaining on us. The light from their torch was getting brighter all the time. Their loud breathing and shouting were just a short distance behind us.

We were approaching the marshy bog now. Clarence and I ran down the embankment into the clearing. Edward was right on our heels with the barking dog in his arms.

It was at that moment that all three of us saw the eerie, flickering flame hanging over the marsh. We stopped dead in our tracks. Our pursuers apparently saw the ball of light, too, because they stopped where they were—just steps behind us. Even Jiggs sensed something unusual was taking place, because he abruptly stopped barking.

"It's the will-o'-the-wisp!" I whispered. "Have you ever seen anything so strange?"

The wavering light hovered over the marshy bog, flaring brightly, then nearly fading away, before flaring again. When it began to move, it seemed to be beckoning us to follow it.

We watched the light for what seemed an eternity. Finally, Clarence whispered, "We can't stand here all night. It can't hurt us. It's just a light. Come on. Let's make a run for it."

"I'm with you," Edward responded. "Let's go!"

When the two of them began to move again, I took off with them. And so did the hobos. The floating flame ahead of us also appeared to be moving faster now. It was leading us in the direction of home.

This can't be happening, I thought. There is no way a light can lead people! Just as that idea flashed through my mind, the light stopped abruptly—right in the middle of the tracks. When it stopped, so did we. So, of course, did our pursuers. We were standing in a line along the edge of the railroad tracks.

And that's when we saw the other light. It was not a flickering, elusive light, but rather a steady, bright beam, moving in our direction from down the tracks. The light appeared to be getting larger and brighter by the second. We knew it was not a regular train, for there was no sound. Just the light!

We tried to run, but our feet seemed to be frozen to the ground. We tried to move away, to dodge the light, but we couldn't seem to budge. The light was getting closer now, headed right for us.

Not a sound did it make in the darkness, this mysterious light in the night. Not a sound did we hear in the darkness, but brighter it grew. So bright!

It swept down the tracks right at us. The light was brighter than day! We knew when it hit, we'd be done for! There was no way to escape! No way!

As we stood there, spellbound, the refrain we had heard at the party earlier ran through my mind: "Swooping you off in the darkness, swooping you off in the night, swooping you off forever, never again to see light!"

It was nearly upon us before we realized that the light *was* attached to something. What was it?

Why, it was a train — a soundless, almost-invisible train.

Then, just before it struck, I heard the sound. It was the eeriest sound I had ever heard in my life. It was not just a train whistle. It was a sad, mournful wail, crying in the night. It was the sound of the mystery train!

CHAPTER 6

It all happened so fast! One minute we were standing beside the railroad tracks, and the next minute we had been swept on board a shadowy car on a fast-moving passenger train.

We looked at each other in disbelief! How could three people have been magically transported inside a speeding vehicle, just like that? Without being hurt in any way?

The three of us stood in a huddle between the seats, gripping each other's hands. As I looked around, I saw our reflections in the windows of this strange railroad car.

First. I saw Edward, looking like a miniature captain of a pirate ship, holding a three-legged black-and-white terrier in his arms. Jiggs, once again, was unexplainably quiet. His tongue was hanging out, and he was panting in short, shallow breaths.

Next in the aisle, I saw the reflection of a tall, thin girl with disheveled hair, wearing a dilapidated-looking paper crown that was tilted to one side. The blue velvet dress was several sizes too large and hung in a most peculiar, almost comical, way. In the reflection, I could see the China doll in my arms.

Clarence was next in the lineup. He looked like a young hobo in a sloppy shirt and ragged-looking pants. A floppy hat sat perched on his head, and a lighted lantern swung from his hand. The lantern was giving enough light inside the train car for us to see.

But, as I looked further down the aisle, I saw, much to my alarm, that Clarence wasn't the only hobo on the train. Behind us stood two other hobos. Yes, Scottie and Smokey Joe had, strangely enough, been swooped up onto the mysterious, fast-moving train, as well! And Joe was still holding his torch! For the moment, the two men were as quiet as we were.

The five of us just stood there, swaying with the movement of the train, looking dumbly at our surroundings and at each other. So far, nobody had spoken a word.

In the dim lantern light I could see straight wooden bench-type seats on both sides of the aisle. The crude benches faced each other. They were all empty.

The next thing I observed was that the floor was made of rough lumber. There were large cracks between the boards. Many of the windows were draped with black cloth. The entire train car reminded me of a hearse back home, the kind that was brought around when somebody died.

We stood in silence for what seemed an eternity. Jiggs, once again, brought us out of our speechless state. He started whimpering. Strange sounds came from his throat. It sounded like a baby crying.

"Clarence . . . Edward . . ." I whispered. "Since there are empty seats here, we might as well sit down."

Clarence nodded. In the lantern light we could see cobwebs criss-crossing the dusty benches. Spiders scurried to get away from the light. I shuddered as Clarence used the lantern to brush them away. Then he sat down on one seat while Edward and I sat down facing him.

We didn't know what Scottie and Joe might do to us, but we didn't have any choice but to stay where we were. So far, the two of them had remained totally silent.

To our great relief, when we sat down, so did they. They were only a few seats behind us, but, somehow, they didn't look nearly as threatening here on the train as they had appeared just a few minutes ago, when they were chasing us through the woods.

Joe opened one of the windows and pitched the burning torch outside. I was glad, because the smoke was beginning to burn my eyes.

All three of us began to pet Jiggs. It was good to have some place to put our attention. He quit his whining and lay down in Edward's lap. Now, as his whimpering stopped, it was my turn to cry. I leaned my head back against the seat and hugged my doll close to my chest. Tears filled my eyes, but not as a result of the torch's fumes.

I thought of our family, safely asleep in our home somewhere behind us. At the rate of speed the train was traveling, home was quickly becoming more distant with each passing minute. How would we ever get back there? I wondered. Were we truly going to a place of darkness, never again to see light? At that moment, I heard the dismal sound of the train whistle somewhere ahead of us. It was a long sad cry, wailing into the night.

We sat in silence for quite a while, staring out the windows into the darkness. Occasionally, we could make out a farmhouse with a light shining, or we realized we were streaking through a small village or town, but we did not see another train. Nor did we hear one. Only the occasional wail of our own train whistle could be heard in this otherwise soundless, gently swaying world of the mystery train.

Edward leaned his head on my shoulder. I thought he had gone to sleep. Suddenly, from out of the clear blue, he said my name. "Emma Mae."

Since I was sitting here in this silent, spider-filled train car with two possible killers behind me, the sudden sound of his voice startled me. I jumped! For some reason, this seemed funny to all three of us. We began to laugh quietly, which helped break the tension.

About this time, we began to hear another sound. One of the hobos behind us had begun to snore softly. We thought that was funny, too.

Edward was sitting straight up now. "I was just wonderin', Sis, since you're the one in the family with the big imagination, have you figured out where we are and where we might be goin'?"

"I don't have a clue, Ed," I said, shaking my head slowly. "How about you Clarence? Got any bright ideas?"

"Not the foggiest," he said, shaking his head, too.

He had turned the knob on the lantern until the wick was barely sticking out, allowing it to produce only a dim light. It was still enough that we could see each other in the darkness.

"Actually, I do have one idea," I whispered. "I think it's time for somebody to start checking things out."

"What do you suggest we do, Emma Mae? Go out and explore the train?" Clarence asked.

"Why not?" I answered. "We surely aren't going to find out anything unless we do, are we?"

"Are you volunteering to go?" he asked.

"I was just wondering," I said, looking around. Now there were two distinct snores coming from the seats behind us.

"Somehow, I'm not worried about Scottie and Smokey Joe just now. So far, they've been totally quiet. And they're temporarily out of commission." I gestured with my head. We all snickered at the snoozing sounds coming from the hobos.

"Why don't I stay here and keep Jiggs and our other things while you two go out sneaking around? Since we haven't seen or heard from anybody so far, I'm sure I'll be all right until you get back."

"What do you think, Ed?" Clarence patted Edward on the knee. "Are you willing to go on an expedition?"

"Of course, I am," he responded, sticking out his chest. "I didn't get to be the captain of a sailin' vessel because I was a coward, you know." He thumped himself on his chest with his fists.

"Okay. Let's do it," Clarence whispered. He stood up, and handed me the lantern. Edward carefully placed the sleeping dog in my lap. Jiggs barely moved. Clarence pointed with his hand. "All right, captain," he whispered. "Lead the way."

Edward stood up, too, and looked up at our big brother. "Wait a minute," he said in a loud whisper. "Since I'm the captain here, *I'm* the one who gives the orders. *You* lead the way."

"Oh, all right," Clarence agreed, moving out into the aisle. "You sure you'll be okay here, Your Majesty?" he asked, removing his floppy hat and bowing to me.

"Quite frankly, I'm not sure about anything," I said softly, "but I think an exploration is our first step. So, begone, you knaves." I gestured dramatically in the direction of the door that led toward the front of the train. "Explore!" But in a quieter voice I added, "But be quick about it!"

During this little interchange, both of the hobos behind us continued to snore, louder than ever.

The two boys tiptoed out of the small circle of light. Suddenly Edward stopped. "Hold on! How are we gonna be able to see anything without a light?"

"Our eyes will adjust to the darkness, my captain," Clarence whispered. "And, besides, a light might just call attention to our investigation."

"All right, if you say so," Edward agreed reluctantly. As they moved through the door into the next car, I heard Edward's muffled voice say, "Here, let me hold onto you. I can't see a thing."

When the door clicked shut, I was left in total silence, except for the snoozing sounds behind me. I barely breathed. I didn't want to do anything to awaken these men while my brothers were away.

The bench felt hard beneath me as I held the lantern, the doll, and the dog. My mind kept replaying the events of the evening just past, especially the part where the stranger had told us about the mystery train.

What could it all mean? I asked myself. Where had the man come from, and where had he gone after he had given that frightening warning of doom? What could be the meaning of his final words, "Never again to see light?"

The swaying of the silent train on the tracks had just about put me to sleep when the boys came tiptoeing back into the patch of light where I sat. They plopped down in the seat facing me.

"You'll never believe what we just saw," Clarence began, shaking his head.

"You'll never believe it," Edward repeated. He was shaking his head just like Clarence.

"Well, don't keep me in suspense," I whispered. "What is it that I won't believe? Where are we? What's going on? Where are we headed?"

"Slow down, Sis," Clarence said in a soft voice. "One thing at a time." He and Edward exchanged looks. Then Clarence began.

"We're on a dilapidated, wooden train with a few other passenger cars that are filled with people. Since they were all asleep, nobody noticed us."

"You should have heard the racket, though, Emma Mae," laughed Edward. "If you think this car is noisy, you should hear the rest of the train!"

Clarence continued, nodding his head and smiling. "As I said, we walked through the cars unnoticed, but we did find out a few things. First, there's one car near the front, just behind the engine, that looks like it would be very nice. It had a light glowing inside, so we figured it was for special people and not for folks like us. Since we couldn't go all the way to the front, we don't know how the train is powered or who is driving it." Clarence stopped and looked at Edward. "Anything else, Ed?"

"Just one thing we haven't told you," Edward added, "and this is the strangest part." He paused and looked me in the eye.

"Yes, yes," I prodded. "Go on. Tell me the strange part."

Again, the two boys exchanged looks. Then they said, in unison, "They're all hobos."

"What do you mean, they're all hobos?"

"That's right, Emma Mae," Clarence said. "Every passenger on this train appears to be a hobo. They all look like homeless travelers. Hobos!"

"But why?" I asked. "How? Where are they going? Why are *we* here with them?" Then I asked the question aloud that I had been asking myself over and over: "What does it all mean?"

Just as I asked that question, we heard it again—the plaintive, mournful whistle—wailing in the night.

CHAPTER 7

We sat in silence for several minutes, thinking about what the boys had discovered.

"You know," I said at last, "since all we have are questions with no answers, I suggest we try to rest a bit. When the answers start arriving, we'll have a lot of things to deal with."

"*Ja*, I agree," Clarence said. "It's been a long day. A little shut-eye will feel good."

"That goes for me, too," said Edward. He reached over and stroked the dog sleeping in my lap. Jiggs simply squirmed a little when Ed touched him, but remained asleep.

Clarence turned the knob on the lantern until the wick disappeared and the flame sputtered out, putting us in total darkness. As our eyes grew accustomed to the darkness, we each squirmed around until we got as comfortable as possible on the rough wooden benches. Soon the boys were asleep. I couldn't relax at first because of all the unanswered questions that were whirling inside my head, but, after a while, I, too, joined the others in sleep.

I don't know how long we slept, but the next thing I knew, someone was saying in a loud, raspy voice, "Man, oh, man! Just look at that!"

I sat straight up, startled. I opened my eyes and looked around. It took a minute for me to remember where I was, but as soon as I saw my two brothers sitting in the seat across from me, looking wild-eyed, it quickly came back to me. We were on a strange, nearly invisible train, mysteriously zipping along the tracks to an unknown destination.

Suddenly, it occurred to me that I could actually *see* everything around me. While it was still a dim light, I realized that it was daybreak. We had slept until dawn! "We made it to see light," I whispered.

We all turned and looked in the direction of the loud voice that had so rudely awakened us moments before. It belonged to Smokey Joe, the hobo with the stubby black whiskers. He was standing in the aisle, bending over, as he looked out the window on the opposite side of the train car.

The sun was barely peeping over the horizon, but what we saw silhouetted in that sunrise was another surprise. There were tall buildings everywhere. I had never seen such tall buildings in my life! And so many of them! They looked as though they could reach up and touch the sky.

"Skyscrapers," Clarence whispered in awe. "I never thought I'd see a real skyscraper in my entire lifetime." At school we had learned about skyscrapers and how they were built. I remembered that the first skyscraper in the world was built in Chicago about thirty years ago.

Many other structures stood between these tall buildings, with streets crisscrossing everywhere. And there were railroad tracks! I had never even imagined there could be so many railroad tracks in one place. Here and there, I saw another train, but it was hard to see anything well, because our own mysterious train streaked along at the same speed it had been going all night.

Behind us Scottie was muttering to himself. "ChiCAgo!" he mumbled with distaste in his voice. "Hate this city, I do. Neverr wanted t' see this ugly place again as long as I lived."

In practically no time at all, we had moved out to the edge of town, passing through the outskirts at lightning speed. It was then that we saw something else we'd never seen before. A huge body of water had come into view on the east side of the train.

Edward exclaimed, "Look at that pond out yonder! Just *look* at that pond. It sure is a big one!!"

The water went on and on, as far as our eyes could see. A large ship was silhouetted on the horizon. Sailboats were tied up to their docks. Fishing boats moved across the water.

Clarence said, "If that was Chicago, then this has to be Lake Michigan. Man! You're right, Ed, It sure *is* a big one!" He slapped Edward on the back.

Scottie was still mumbling in his seat behind us. "Outta therre, we arre, and good rrriddance, too," he said.

Joe, who hadn't said anything at all since he first awakened us, sat back down across from his companion. He looked as though he felt terrible.

I turned in my seat and, for the first time, looked into the faces of the two men. After all, the five of us had shared a train car for a whole night, and nothing serious had happened. Actually, nothing had happened at all. There had been no communication. Now I thought it was time to break the ice.

"*Guten Morgen,*" I said to them in German. I smiled. Somehow these two men looked as harmless as two fleas sitting there on the wooden train seat.

"And good mornin' to you, me lass," Scottie said, returning my smile. Joe just frowned. He didn't seem to be in a very good mood.

Edward and Clarence followed my lead. They stood on either side of me. Scottie stood up and nodded at us.

"I believe some of us 'ave met beforre," he said. "If I rememberr, ye be Mae and Ed's childrrren." It was a relief to know that he was actually acquainted with our parents, whose names are Mae and Ed.

"*Ja,* that's right," I said. "Edward and I have seen you plenty of times in our neighborhood. This is our older brother, Clarence."

He reached to shake Clarence's hand. "And it's pleased I be to make yourr acquaintance, me lad."

Clarence returned the handshake, "Nice to meet you, too," he said politely.

Joe had remained seated during this conversation.

"We know you, too, Mr. Joe," Edward commented. "We've seen you lots of times, walking up and down the railroad tracks."

Joe smiled a lopsided grin. "I knows most of yer fam'ly since I hang around there so much," he said. "Good people, ye b'long to. Good people." He nodded his head in approval. Joe hadn't stood up as he said this, but remained seated on the bench seat. He continued in his raspy voice, "Ye'll hafta excuse me fer not standin' up, but I ain't feelin' too good this mornin'."

He chuckled to himself. "Fer a train-hoppin' hobo, I'm a'feared I'm a terrible traveler. I git sick to my stomach if I stay on a movin' train too long. An' the way I see it, this here ride's been a waaay too long."

Since the two men were acting so normally this morning, I felt encouraged to ask the question that was bothering me.

"Now that we've all greeted each other, could I please ask a question?"

"Surrre, me bonny lass. Ask what ye please," Scottie responded.

"Well, last night . . . ah . . . that is, yesterday . . ." I wasn't quite sure how to get into asking them about what had happened in the woods.

I didn't have a chance to pursue the subject further, though, because, at that very moment, the door at the end of the train car banged open. A person came walking in. Quickly, we turned and sat back down in our seats. The new arrival was a man dressed in a brown business suit with a white shirt and bow tie. He had a black derby hat perched on top of his head. A cigar dangled from his lips.

He swaggered up the aisle to where we sat. When he got even with our seat, he looked directly at us for the first time. He stopped short. His eyes grew big and his mouth flew open in a loud gasp. His cigar tumbled to the floor. For several seconds he just stood there, staring at first one of us and then another. Then, in a coarse whisper, he asked, "What . . . are you children . . . doing here?"

We all three just looked back at him with blank looks on our faces, exchanging stares of disbelief.

Finally, I said, "You're asking *us*? That's the same question we were planning to ask *you*!"

Just then Jiggs, who had been sleeping in the seat, raised his head and looked at the man who was standing in front of us. He reacted exactly the same way he had at the party the night before. He bared his teeth and started barking ferociously; for Jiggs, like the rest of us, had recognized the storyteller from the Halloween party.

"Quiet, Jiggs," I demanded, trying desperately to hold onto the small animal who was barking loudly and straining to get away from me.

"Here, let me have 'im," Edward said. He got Jiggs in his arms and started stroking him, talking softly in his ear. Jiggs immediately settled down.

The man, who had drawn away from the barking dog, moved back up beside us. "I can't believe this. I just can't believe it," he said with his strange accent, shaking his head. His gaze went further down the car beyond us to where Smokey Joe and Scottie sat.

"Now you two blokes are okay here. This is where you belong." He looked at us again and shook his head. "But the *children*. I don't know how this has happened. We've never taken *children* before." He pulled a white handkerchief from his coat pocket. He lifted his hat and blotted perspiration from his brow. "I think we've got ourselves a little problem here," he said, more to himself than to anyone else.

Clarence, who had been quietly observing the scene, stood and began to dance his soft-shoe shuffle in the aisle. Then he stopped and bowed.

"Clarence, here, sir," he said. "Correct me if I'm wrong, but I thought you just said that you have yourself a little problem. We are probably confused, but all night long we've been telling ourselves that *we* were the ones with a problem. Perhaps you can explain it for us. Who has the problem—you or us?"

The man continued to stand there, staring at us. He looked first at Clarence, standing in the aisle; then at Edward with the now-quiet dog in his arms; and, finally, at me, holding my China doll.

"*Children*," he said again. "I just can't believe this has happened."

"Well, sir," Clarence said, as he bent over and picked up the man's cigar. He went into his tap dance routine again. "You can take it from us, something has definitely happened, because . . ." he did another shuffle with his feet, "here *we* are, and here is your cigar."

This time as he finished the little dance routine, he held his hand out toward the stranger in the brown suit. In his hand was the cigar. The man reached for it, put it in his mouth, and began stroking his chin.

"Hmmm," he said, "you're good at that. It seems to me I've seen . . . wait a minute . . . the Halloween party last night at that little train station!"

Now he seemed to be getting excited.

"Yes, yes," he said, starting to smile. "The dancing hobo with the little dancing dog. Is this the three-legged dog that dances?" he asked, looking more closely at Jiggs.

As he leaned to get a better look at Jiggs, the little dog bared his teeth and started growling. Edward whispered in his ear again to quiet him.

The man was getting more excited.

"And you," he said, pointing at Edward, "you're the one who plays the harmonica so well. What an act! Why, you'll make a great addition to the show! What a stroke of luck for me!" Then he added, "I went to that little party last night looking for hobos to join our group. I didn't find any hobos there, but instead I found a brand new act!"

He glanced behind us to where Scottie and Joe still remained quietly seated. "And, somehow, I got me some new hobos, to boot! What a fantastic stroke of luck!"

Now the man really smiled. He clasped his hands together in front of him and rubbed them, back and forth, the way greedy people do when they are scheming to make money. Only then did he look at me.

"What about you, young lady. Where do you fit into all this? I've seen what the boys can do. What can *you* do for me?"

As I sat there watching this man, it occurred to me that something was terribly wrong. My attention was first drawn to it by the way Jiggs had reacted, both last night and again this morning. Jiggs had *never* growled like that before in his entire life.

The more I observed, the more I realized that something bad was about to happen. I also felt that the bad something would be connected to this man in the brown suit. So I reacted.

"Well," I said quietly. "The first thing I can do is to ask *you* a few questions—like, where are we? What kind of train are we on? Where are we going? How do you plan to get us back home? What kind of show are you talking about?"

As the questions started spilling from my mouth, I stood up, moving closer and closer to the man. By the time I had asked that last question, I was practically in his face. It was obvious that I was angry as my voice was getting louder and louder.

He started backing away from me down the aisle toward the door. Apparently, he had never dealt with an angry twelve-year-old girl before. I knew I had him squirming, so I kept at it.

"That's not all I want to know. Who are *you*? And who are all these people on this train? Where are you taking them? And what did you mean last night when you said, 'Never again to see light?'"

I continued moving toward the man as he backed farther down the aisle. I didn't know what the others were thinking or doing, but I was upset with this stranger and I really didn't care what they thought.

"And in case you're wondering, that's just the beginning of my questions," I said in a voice that had grown very loud.

The man looked flustered, but he finally found his own voice. "Just a minute, young lady. You can't push me around like this," he said, putting his hands up in front of him with his palms facing outward. I took his gesture as a threat, and, in my anger, decided to go one step further.

"I believe your first question to me was to ask what I can do for you." I moved even closer to him.

"Here is one thing I can do!"

And with that, I raised my foot up and brought it down sharply on top of the toes of his right foot. I was glad in that moment that I still had on my Sunday shoes and was not barefooted.

"Yeow!" yelled the man in the brown suit as he reached down and grabbed his foot.

"You . . . you . . . you'll pay for that, young lady." He had been caught completely off guard. He didn't know what to do.

He turned abruptly and rushed toward the door. He looked back and shook his cigar at me. "You don't just stomp on my foot and not pay for it!" he said as he hurried out of the car. "You'll pay!" The door slammed shut behind him.

Then, for the first time since daybreak, we heard the train whistle again. Even in broad, open daylight, chills ran up and down my spine.

As I turned to go back to my seat, I was greeted with applause. All four of the other occupants of the train car were standing and clapping their hands. Even Smokey Joe.

"I'm sorry, fellows," I said. "I don't know what came over me just now, but . . . I guess . . . " I hesitated, then said in a high-pitched, quavery voice ". . . the 'willer-de-wisp' tole me to . . . the 'willer-de-wisp' tole me to."

Edward and Clarence laughed loudly.

We all sat down in our seats again. "I'll probably be sorry I went after him like that, but I have a bad feeling about all this."

"We'll take up for you, Sis," Clarence said in an unexpected, but kindly way. "I don't feel good about it, either."

Scottie called out from his seat, "Just rremind me neverr to get ye upset with me," he laughed. "But me thinks ye were about to ask a question a bit ago when we were interrrupted," he went on. "What was it?"

Before I had a chance to answer, we had another interruption. This time it was the sudden slowing of the train.

We looked out the windows. Instead of just a blurred landscape whizzing past on the left hand side of the tracks, at this slower speed, we could actually see the view. The farmland scenery looked like paintings in a picture book. Every farmhouse had a dairy barn with silos. Herds of black and white cows grazed in pastures. With the autumn foliage on the trees, it was simply beautiful.

On the right side of the tracks, the colorful trees hugged the shores of Lake Michigan. The lake had rarely been out of our sight since we left Chicago. Sunbeams on the water's surface did a soft-shoe shuffle of their own, as they reflected brightly in the ripples on the water.

Now that we were moving more slowly, we could also read signboards along the right side of the railroad tracks. One of the signs read "Racine."

"Clarence," I said when I saw it, "do you think we could be coming into Racine, Wisconsin? Don't we have relatives who live in Racine?"

Clarence nodded. "It seems like I've heard Mama talk about her sister who moved to Wisconsin when she got married a long time ago."

Edward added, "When I brought the milk bucket in the kitchen one day last week, Mama was reading a letter. I asked her about it, and she said it was a letter from her sister who had moved away from Kentucky many years ago. She had tears in her eyes when she talked about it. I picked up the envelope and saw the return address. It was Racine, Wisconsin. I remember it because it had such pretty handwriting."

As our train slowed down even more, we saw many railroad tracks running alongside each other. Various kinds of train cars could be seen.

"Look," Edward said excitedly, "look at those bright-colored cars. That looks like a circus train!" We looked in the direction he was pointing. He was right. We were pulling alongside a long circus train, complete with animal cages and boxcars.

Our train had slowed to a crawl by now. All of a sudden, from somewhere up ahead, there came a strange hissing sound, immediately followed by an abrupt forward lurch. Then stillness.

"Do you think we've come to the end of the line?" I asked quietly.

From somewhere in front of us, the train wailed two short blasts: "Hoooo! Hoooo!" Then . . . silence.

CHAPTER 8

Our suddenly still world didn't last long, because the man in the brown suit came rushing through the door again. Jiggs started his usual growling sounds at the sight of him.

"Okay! Okay! Come on! Follow me!" he ordered in his strange accent. "All of you. Everybody out!" He gestured with his hand.

We didn't think we had a choice so all five of us did as we were told. We picked up our belongings and followed him. As we walked into the car in front of us, we saw that we were at the rear of a long line of men, who all looked a lot like Smokey Joe. And even smelled like Smokey Joe, I noticed!

The next thing I observed was that none of them talked. It was a silent procession, moving down the aisle of the train. Since we were at the rear of the group, we followed along to the exit. As we stepped down onto the platform of the railway station, Edward said softly, "Look at the train."

We turned to look at the mysterious train that had brought us screaming through the night to this distant place. Except for the engine and first car, the rest of the cars looked like they had been built from old boards, roughly nailed together. But the oddest thing was, while we could see it, we could *barely* see it. "It seems like more of an impression than a real train," I whispered to my brothers. "Why, it's almost invisible."

Suddenly, while we stood there looking at it, the strangest thing happened. It vanished! Disappeared! Right before our eyes!

"What the . . .!" Edward exclaimed.

He ran back and stood in the middle of the tracks, rubbing his eyes in disbelief. There was not a single train car in sight! The three of us looked at each other in amazement, but we were the only ones standing there gaping at the empty space.

A short distance away at the edge of the crowd, I spotted a tall man in a striped cap. He looked like a train engineer. He, too, was looking at the railroad tracks. He had an unusual-looking stick in his hand that was pointed toward the tracks. As I watched, he put the stick in the pocket of his coveralls, then turned, and walked quickly away. Before I could tell my brothers to look, he was gone.

The rest of the passengers gathered in the center of the platform in a large, silent group. I guessed there must have been seventy-five to eighty men. The man in the brown suit walked to the front of the crowd, and turned to face us. I smiled smugly when I noticed he walked with a slight limp. In his hand he held a large, black megaphone that he put to his mouth. He began to speak loudly into it.

"Since most of you have been here before, you are aware of our practice. Every time the train goes out on a run in search of new recruits, we all go out with it. Then we all return," he said in his unusual accent. "For that reason, you already know what is expected of you. We do have new volunteers, however, so I'll go over the rules for their benefit."

"Do you think he's callin' us volunteers?" Edward asked quietly. "I don't remember anybody askin' if we wanted to come here."

"Quiet in the back, there!" the man bellowed into the megaphone. "From now on, there will be *no talking* among yourselves when we are all gathered together," he commanded sternly. "That's rule No. 1."

"Rule No. 2: You will always follow the directions of your leaders. Offenders will be taken to yonder prison and locked up." He pointed to a tall stone structure in the distance that had turrets. These small towers gave it a castle-like appearance.

"Rule No. 3: With the exception of our new volunteers, the rest of you already know what your jobs are. For the new people, you will soon be given your work assignments. You'll be expected to perform your duty and perform it well. Or else!"

Or else what, I wondered; but I didn't dare ask.

"Finally," he rumbled into the megaphone, "the guards around you are armed and prepared, as always, to take you prisoner or shoot you, should you not cooperate. Do you have any questions?"

I had about a million questions, but when I looked around and saw the guards with their eyes scanning the group, I decided this was not the time or place to ask them. I would just go along with the group to see what would happen next.

My brothers and I exchanged looks of uncertainty as we shrugged our shoulders. But, believe me, we didn't say a word! Even Jiggs was unusually quiet at the moment.

Another man, wearing a black top hat, had arrived to stand beside the man in the brown suit. Once again, the first man put the megaphone to his mouth and boomed, "Sergeant Lorrie and I will lead you to your quarters now. Follow us."

The two leaders turned to lead the way. The strange-looking group of people began moving after them. I looked around to see that Scottie and Joe were following the rest of the crowd. The guards, with their guns pointed skyward, kept an alert watch over the entire group.

As we trailed along behind, I couldn't help but notice the strange movements of the men in the group. They just didn't look right out of their eyes, as Papa would say. There was no vitality, no sparkle. It was almost as if they were wind-up toys like the ones we sometimes got for Christmas—the kind you have to wind up with a key in its back in order to make it move.

There was one person, though, who seemed different. He didn't fit the mold of a typical tramp or hobo. He was wearing a hat. A pair of small glasses perched on his nose. There was an air of self-confidence about him that seemed to be lacking among the others. He kept looking around at us, smiling slightly.

As the procession moved off the platform, we trudged along behind. We had walked only a short distance before we made a sharp turn to our left. The prison we had seen earlier from the train station was on the right side of the walkway. Up close, it looked even more like a castle that had been lifted out of a book of fairy tales. Unlike a storybook castle, though, this one had armed guards walking back and forth outside the gates.

A large white house stood next to the castle. It reminded me of the Dexter house back at Krebs Station, where the Halloween party had taken place last night. Just beyond the white house, we came to a tall brick wall with several strands of barbed wire twisted together along the top. A wide gate in this wall had armed guards stationed at each side.

As we passed through the gate, I looked around. A shiver ran down my spine. Why, I thought, even though this is not the prison building, in reality, we will still be prisoners.

Colorful tents of red, yellow, and blue formed a semi-circle in the space inside the walls. In the center of this half-circle, at the far side, was a long black tent. It was much larger than the others. As we stood waiting for our assignments, a young girl with a basket came out of the black tent. She walked in our direction. She had to stop and wait for our group to move before she could pass through the gate to leave.

The girl appeared to be about my age and size. Actually, I thought she looked a lot like me. When she saw my China doll, she looked up at me in surprise. Our eyes met. She raised her eyebrows and smiled, a questioning kind of smile. I smiled in return as she went on through the gate.

The person referred to as Sergeant Lorrie stood at the gate entrance and checked names off a list as each person in the group filed past him. He was a tall, thin man, dressed in a black cutaway coat and striped black pants, along with the black top hat. He carried a black walking cane. His long, thin mustache curled up at each end.

Now that most of the hobos ahead of us were moving on to their quarters, I saw Sergeant Lorrie hand slips of paper to both Scottie and Joe. As he did so, he said something to them. They stepped over to the side and looked around at us.

Since we were at the back of the line, the sergeant hadn't gotten a good look at us until we were almost in front of him. "Ah, ha," he smiled a phony-looking smile. "You must be the newest volunteers. The *children*! I've been hearing all about you from Major Andrews."

So now we knew the name of the man in the brown suit. He was *Major* Andrews, which, obviously, meant that he was a superior officer with some kind of authority.

"Now that you've joined our ranks," the sergeant said, "I want to extend a special welcome to you." Up close like this I saw that he had an artificial-looking smile pasted on his face. His eyes darted back and forth in quick movements, like he wanted to see everything going on around him at once. Our Papa would say he had shifty eyes.

I felt an immediate distrust of this man. Apparently, Jiggs shared my feelings because he bared his teeth and made growling sounds. It was the same reaction he had shown each time he had encountered Major Andrews. Edward whispered in his ear and stroked his head to keep him quiet.

"Since we have never had children before," he began, "we haven't quite decided what to do with you boys. The young lady's assignment was easy, though." He looked at me, smiling that fake smile and fluttering his eyelashes. "You'll be working for the kitchen patrol."

"The what?" I asked.

He fluttered his eyelashes again. "The kitchen patrol. That's the group of people who help with kitchen duties. It's called KP for short."

He turned and pointed with his cane toward the long black tent. "That tent over there is our mess hall or eating place. That's where all the food for our volunteers is prepared and served. You'll be given tasks each day to assist the cooks. There is a man in charge who will tell you what you'll be expected to do."

He used his cane to point to Smokey Joe. "One of the other new blokes will also be working KP duty. I'm sure the two of you will be able to work together." Joe signaled at me with a little wave of his hand. I smiled back at him.

"There is one more thing, sir, if you please," I said, pulling out my skirt and dipping into a small curtsy.

He whirled around and glared at me. He was not fluttering his eyelashes now.

"What is it?" he asked sharply. This time there was an edge to his voice. He started twirling the ends of his mustache again as he glared at me.

"Is there any place I might be able to get some different clothes? This velvet dress is not exactly what I think I need to wear when I do KD, or whatever it is I'm supposed to be doing."

He sighed and rolled his eyes upward in his head. "That's K*P*! That's the military term for kitchen *patrol!*" He frowned at me for a second, then said, "I see what you mean about the dress, though. I'll see what I can do about it."

He looked at the boys. "As for you two, I'll give you time to get settled in your living quarters before we decide what your jobs will be," he said flatly. "You may be helping that other bloke over there clean the elephant stalls. We'll see."

He pointed with his cane toward Scottie, whose face was red enough to match his beard. He looked very angry.

Just as Sergeant Lorrie finished giving us our assignments, Major Andrews returned. The two of them saluted each other, military style. "At ease, Sergeant," Major Andrews said. They both relaxed with their hands behind their backs.

He looked at our little group. Scottie and Joe had moved back over to stand with us in what seemed to be a protective gesture—an especially kind act for two people who had possibly been killers the day before.

The hobo with the hat and glasses, who had smiled at us earlier, was standing not far away, watching; but he wasn't smiling now.

Major Andrews came to stand in front of us. He took his derby hat off and placed it under his arm. Then he leaned over and looked directly in our faces. "There are a few things I want to be sure you understand. While I realize you didn't ask to come here, the five of you were selected to serve as the newest members of our team by the train engineer, General Rankin. Now that you are here, you will do as you are instructed under all circumstances, whether you like it . . . or not!" He looked specifically at me when he made that last statement.

"You are never to attempt to leave the premises without permission from one of the officers. Furthermore, you will be constantly watched when you are at work. We run a tight ship around here, and we expect *complete* cooperation from every person on our team." Again he glared at me. "Now," he paused in his delivery of the stern instructions, "do you have any questions?"

"I do, sir," Edward said. As he said this, he clicked his heels together, stood at attention, and saluted. Major Andrews actually let a small smile spread across his face.

"At ease, private," he said.

"I know I am just a little kid who hasn't been around much, but my sister asked some questions earlier that haven't been answered yet. It would help us to know – like, where are we? What are we doin' here? And how are we goin' to get back home?"

"All right, private," Major Andrews responded with a sigh. "Those are good questions. Let me see if I can answer them. As I said earlier, when I went to the Halloween party at that train station in West Kentucky last night, I was hoping to get some new volunteers. I wasn't looking for child recruits, but for good prospects to come to work for us here at the circus—you know, people like these two fellows here." He pointed at Scottie and Joe.

He continued. "We are all a part of the famous circus that you may or may not have seen in your town in the past. For the moment, we're stationed here in this small city in Wisconsin. We use this as our main headquarters so that we can take the circus out to the surrounding cities and towns, especially Milwaukee, which is not far away.

"Every year we come here. This is our home, so to speak, for the summer and fall. All of us do our share of the work. In return, our volunteers get room and board, which means they have a place to stay and have food to eat."

Major Andrews continued to look each one of us in the eye as he talked. I was reminded that he had a very good way of capturing his audience. "As for your last question . . . " now he paused and, I thought, sighed slightly, " . . . how are you going to get back home? I regret to tell you this, private, but, from now on, this *is* your home. Once you come here, you stay forever. And that's final!"

With that, he turned sharply toward Sergeant Lorrie and said, "All right, Sergeant. They have been properly briefed. You may proceed in getting them settled in their living quarters."

And, with that, the two men saluted each other. Major Andrews pulled a fresh cigar out of his pocket. He put it in his mouth, then turned and glared at me before he walked away.

"Okay, okay! Let's move it!" Sergeant Lorrie barked. "You've received your orders, but you are to stay in your tent until further notice. Let's go! Let's go!" he ordered. "Move it on out! Over to the blue tent on the far left. That's the one the five of you and the mutt are going to share." And, with that, he turned and walked away, joining Major Andrews as they strolled toward the gate.

So we were to be sharing a tent with two people who had possibly terrible motives that we didn't even know about. People that, only yesterday, had been mysteriously burying something . . . or somebody . . . in our woods. But, somehow, instead of feeling frightened, I felt a sense of relief. It seemed to me that, under the circumstances, Scottie and Joe were not the bad guys here.

The five of us continued to watch in silence as the sergeant and major strutted across the grounds on their way toward the entrance. They saluted the guards who stood at attention with their guns resting on their shoulders. We watched as they walked out the main gate and across to the large white house with the front porch and white picket fence. The prison loomed like a castle beside it. The two of them patted each other on the back and laughed loudly as they climbed the steps and disappeared inside the house.

No, I thought as we turned to walk toward our tent. Scottie and Joe were definitely not the bad guys here.

CHAPTER 9

"So this is going to be our *new home*," groaned Clarence as we walked toward the blue tent.

Edward, always the explorer, ran ahead. "It looks bigger up close than it did from back there," he called. "And look! Instead of a tent flap it's got a real wooden door set in a doorframe."

He knocked on the door, tilting his head to listen for a response. "Anybody home?" he hollered. Naturally, since there was no response, he opened the door and popped inside. Clarence, Jiggs, and I were right on his heels.

I was pleasantly surprised by the layout. "It looks bigger inside than I expected," I commented. The center of the tent was an open area. A small table with four chairs filled the middle of the space. Then four compartments branched out from this open space like spokes on a wheel. Edward darted in and out of each tiny cubicle, checking it all out.

I pulled up a flap and looked inside one of the compartments. "They sure didn't spend much money on furniture, did they? Just one single cot in each room."

Edward said, "But at least we have pillows and blankets, so I guess it could be a whole lot worse."

Clarence had been quiet during this exploration stage. He walked around and looked into each of the cubicles.

"Well," he said, "according to my mathematical calculations, it's pretty hard to divide five evenly into four. So what do you think? How are we going to divide the five of ourselves up into four rooms?"

Quickly, Edward responded, "I know. Jiggs and I can share space with you, big brother. We don't mind sleeping on the floor, do we, Jiggs?" He leaned over and scratched his little dog's head. "Think the three of us can bunk together?"

"Fine with me," Clarence agreed. "Emma Mae? Is that all right with you?"

"Sure," I said agreeably. "Why not? Maizey and I can share our own private space."

By this time Smokey Joe and Scottie had joined us inside our tent home. As I looked at the two of them here in the semi-darkness inside the tent, they looked much scarier than they had outside in the sunlight.

Clarence turned to the two men. "Scottie? Joe?" he said. "It looks like you each have your own space. Just take your pick." He gestured to the two remaining rooms.

Scottie took a quick look into both compartments and said, "It don't matterr t'me, as long as I 'ave a place t' lay me head. That's all I need."

Joe said, "It don't matter to me, neither. I'll just tek this one over here. Bad as I feel right now, I'm ready to git me a little shut-eye."

He walked into one of the cubicles and let the door flap close over the opening. But Scottie sat down in one of the chairs in the center chamber.

"I be mighty tirrred meself, but I don't think I could sleep jest yet." He reached in his pocket and pulled out the slip of paper that Mr. Lorrie had handed him earlier. "Cleanin' up after the stinkin' elephants," he grumbled, shaking his head. His face started getting red again. He looked defeated. I couldn't help feeling sorry for him.

Clarence and I sat in two of the other chairs. Finally, Edward, who had run out of places to explore, flopped down, too. He sat in the empty chair nearest the Scotchman. Jiggs jumped up in his lap.

"Mr. Scottie?" Edward said as he stroked his dog, "I heard you say something a little while ago on the train about not likin' Chicago. I believe you said you never wanted to go back there as long as you lived. I was just wonderin' why."

"Well," he began, "it be a long storry, but I guess me got the time t' tell it, and ye've got the time t' listen, if ye be interrested."

"Yes, yes, Scottie," I prodded. "We'd love to hear your story."

And so he began. "I was born in Chicago away back in 1861. Lived with me mither and faither and me wee brothers and sisters. Many other family members lived in the same area. We werre a happy family, we werre, living a bonny life together.

"Then, one night, when I be about ten years old, trragedy strruck. One of me relatives, who lived nearby, had a barn with cows in it. One of the cows kicked over a lighted lantern, and the barn caught a'firre. Before help could come to put it out, the fire began to sprread.

"It's still like a terrible nightmare, even after all these years. I was a'sleepin' in me bed when the raging flames came roarring down upon our home. Everybody ran, scrreaming and calling for help. I don'no why, but for some reason, I escaped. I be the only one of me own family that wasn't killed that night in the Grreat Chicago Fire. About 300 other people died, as well.

"Thousands of people were left homeless, including me. Not a person did I have to take me in, so they sent me to live with me mither's relatives back in the southern part of Scotland."

All the time Scottie was talking, the three of us sat in silence, not saying a word, hardly daring to breathe.

"But try as I might, I have never been able to get the memorry out of me poor head about the terrrible fire. Because of that, I guess, I have never had a job I could hold onto. I came back to Amerrica a few years ago, but still haven't found a place to call me home."

By this time, tears were streaming down Scottie's face. "And herre I be, at age 53, with not a thing to call me own; without even a place to lay me head at night. And now I have to clean up after the stinkin' elephants." He put his face in his hands and sobbed.

Needless to say, the three of us were crying with him. Regardless of what he might have done yesterday, my heart went out to this man who sat weeping with us in the big blue tent. I went to him and put my arms around him, hugging him tightly. He hugged me in return. After a few minutes, his sobs became less. When he grew quiet and had begun to regain his composure, I released my embrace but stayed beside him with my hand on his shoulder.

"Ye know," he said, looking around at us, "that's the first time in m' life that I've been able to talk about the firre and all the terrrible losses and changes it brrought t'me when I was just a lad. Folks tried and tried to get me to talk about it, but, for some reason, I never could, until today."

We waited for him to continue when he was ready. He looked at each of us for a long time. Then he said, "Thank ye, children, for lettin' a worthless man like meself tell his pitiful tale."

"Scottie," I said quietly. I continued to stand close to him. I was thinking hard about all the things I had heard my parents and the people at our church say about things like this. "What makes you think you are worthless? Just because you were a victim of circumstances as a young child doesn't mean you are a worthless person. Why, you have many good qualities," I continued. "I don't know when I've ever met a person who seemed to be more kind and considerate than you have been to us today."

"That's right, Mr. Scottie," Edward added. "And I remember how nice it was for you to help us sort all them potatoes in our backyard last summer, getting them ready to take to market. Why, I'll bet there are lots of things you could teach us—like how to juggle. I'd love to be able to juggle like you do."

"Juggle?" he said. "Do you mean . . . like juggling potatoes?" He did an imitation of juggling with his hands.

"Ja," Edward answered. "Why, you were so good at juggling, you looked like you belonged in a . . . wait a minute! I was just about to say 'circus.' Hey! Maybe that's it!" Edward's voice was getting louder as the idea grew. "Maybe you can get a job here at the circus as a juggler!"

"It would sure beat cleaning up after the stinkin' elephants," Clarence said dryly.

"Be gorry! I think ye may be onto something. At least, it's worth a try. Maybe we can speak to Mr. Lorrrie about it when he returns."

I clapped my hands in excitement. Jiggs, who had been sleeping in Edward's lap, woke up and began to bark. After the tension of the story, we were all ready to find something to celebrate.

"Now," Scottie said, "earlier on the trrain you said you had a question about something that happened yesterrday. We keep gettin' interrupted everrytime you ask. What was it you wanted to know, me lass?"

"Oh, yes. Edward and I were out in the woods late yesterday afternoon when . . . "

But, once again, I was interrupted. Apparently, our noise had awakened Smokey Joe, for we heard him growl in a loud voice: "Hey! Would ye keep it down in there? It's hard fer a bum like me t' sleep with all that noise!"

We all burst into laughter. We were still laughing when there was a sharp rap at the outside door. Our laughter died in our throats as we looked at each other—wondering who would be on the other side.

CHAPTER 10

Edward jumped up to open the door with Jiggs in his arms. When the little dog saw who was standing there, he started barking again. Almost immediately, his barking turned into a snarl. It was Sergeant Lorrie. He stepped into the tent, giving the dog a menacing look. He held two bags in his arms.

"I have the orders for you two boys now," he said, twirling his mustache in that nervous habit of his. "You're to report to the main gate immediately after lunch to go with Major Andrews and myself for an audition. You'll be trying out for a part in the musical clown act in the circus."

"As for you" he turned his stern look on me, "I was able to get you some different clothes. You may not like them, but it was the best I could do." He handed the smaller bag to me. "You'll have the rest of the day off from work today, but you're to report to the mess hall in the morning after you hear Reveille being played."

"Excuse me, sir," I interrupted. "Thank you very much for the clothes, but I'm afraid I don't understand. I go to work after I hear *what* in the morning?"

"Reveille. You know—the wake-up call. It's pronounced 're-vel-lee.' We have a bugle player who plays a tune called Taps at night, as a sign that it's time to turn the lights out and go to bed. He then plays Reveille in the morning, as a signal it's time to get up. It's the military way of keeping everybody on the same schedule. You got that?" he asked.

"Yes, sir," I nodded.

"Now," he went on, looking at Scottie. "You are to begin your job right after breakfast tomorrow morning. There will be an entire group of men deployed to go to the animal area to start the day's work of washing the animals and cleaning the stalls. You will be among them."

"Excuse me again, sir," I said, crossing my fingers behind my back for luck. "We have an idea for something that would . . . " I hesitated for a minute, thinking of how to present the idea of Scottie's juggling ability. Suddenly a light flashed on inside my head, and I continued, ". . . something that would add a great deal of interest to my brothers' act. Mr. Scottie, here, is a very talented juggler."

Clarence picked up on the idea. "That's right, Mr. Lorrie," he said. "While Edward plays the harmonica and Jiggs and I dance, Scottie could juggle all kinds of things around us. It could add a lot of interest to our performance."

Mr. Lorrie stood there twisting his mustache, looking at first one of the would-be performers and then another.

"Hmmm," he said at last, "I can't see anything wrong with trying it. We don't have a clown who can juggle at the moment, so this might work." He began nodding his head up and down.

Scottie smiled. "I'd be mighty grrateful for the chance to give it a trry, sir."

"Very well then," Mr. Lorrie agreed, "All three of you and the dog will need to meet us at the gate after lunch and we'll go over to the big tent for the audition. As for that other oaf," he gestured toward the snoring sounds that were once again coming from the closed cubicle, "he can just wait until tomorrow morning to begin KP with the girl."

And with that, he turned abruptly and walked toward the door. He stopped short, looking down at the bag he was still holding. "Oh, yes," he said. "Here are a pillow and extra blankets for you. Nights get chilly this far north." He dropped the bag on the floor and stepped out of the tent.

He hadn't been gone but a minute or two when the clanging sound of the dinner bell started calling folks to lunch. Just as the bell stopped ringing, we heard a different sound. It was another knock at the door. This time it was a light tapping sound.

I hesitantly opened the door and peeped out. All around the courtyard, men were quietly leaving their tents as they walked toward the mess hall located in the big black tent. Then I realized there was someone standing just outside our own tent door. It was the hobo with the hat and glasses who had been watching us since we first got off the train. His eyes darted nervously around the campground.

"Excuse me, miss, but may I please come in for a minute?" he asked in a quiet voice.

"Sure," I answered, opening the door wider.

He took a quick look at the four of us sitting around the table. In a quiet voice, he said, "I'm probably taking a chance by coming here, but there are several things you need to know about your whereabouts."

He went back to the door and peeked outside; then closed it, and came back over to the table. Edward moved to the floor so the visitor could have a seat.

"First of all, my name is Ronald Wood," he said, placing his hat on the table. "I am a schoolteacher by profession, so I am very fond of children. Actually, I have three of my own back home." Tears sprang to his eyes as he said that. He took his glasses off and dabbed his eyes with a handkerchief. "That's the reason I've come here. I want to warn you of the dangers that are all around."

"What do you mean . . . 'dangers?'" Clarence asked in a surprised voice.

"The people in charge of this 'outfit,' they call it, are untrustworthy scoundrels. They are crooks of the worst kind, because they are dealing with human lives."

He continued, "They have this incredible, magical train which they use to go out and pick up people walking along the railroad tracks at night. They bring them here, and use them for free labor. Then they keep them captive forever, until they die. There is no way to escape!"

"Never again to see light," I whispered, my eyes growing big with comprehension. It was beginning to make sense now.

"But what are the dangers we need to know about?" Clarence asked.

"I'll have to speak quickly," he said, "because it is the lunch hour. As you can hear, people are going to eat now." He pointed his thumb toward the outside sounds. "Nobody is to miss a meal. It's one of the *rules*," he said with contempt. "And herein is a danger I have discovered. I believe I am the only prisoner who knows it."

He crossed to the door and peered out once again. Satisfied that he was still safe with us, he sat back down and whispered, "Don't . . . eat . . . the meat they serve."

"Why not?" Edward asked. He was whispering, too. "I love meat. It's just about my favorite food. That, and dessert."

"Most people are like you. They enjoy having meat with their meals," Ronald said, "which is usually fine; but I have concluded that it's different here."

"Different?" I asked. "Different in what way?"

"Let me explain," Ronald continued. "I think the cooks here are under orders to put something in the meat that affects emotions; that means, the way a person feels about things. The reason I've noticed this is because I'm a vegetarian. I only eat vegetables and fruit. I don't eat meat. I've watched how all the new people who come here seem to be average at first, but they slowly begin to lose their ability to communicate or do things with each other in regular ways. I am the only one who still seems to act in a normal way."

He looked at us and shook his head. "I've thought about it a lot, and have concluded that the only thing different between the rest of the men and me is the fact that they all eat meat and I don't. That's why I feel sure there is something going on with the meat."

"What a mean trick to play on people," Edward said quietly, shaking his head. "Putting stuff in their *meat*."

"I agree with you, young man, but I wonder if any of you have noticed that the prisoners don't interact or talk to each other?"

"They're like wind-up toys," I said. "I noticed that as soon as we got off the train."

Ronald nodded his head. "That's a very good way to put it. They do exactly what they're told to do with no questions asked. It's a bad thing the officers are doing to these people, but I don't know what can be done about it."

Shaking his head again, he sighed and stood up. "Now I've got to get in line before they miss me. If you don't go where you're supposed to go or do what you're supposed to do, they will punish you. That prison you saw earlier today is for real."

Both Clarence and Scottie stood to shake Ronald's hand. "Thank you, sir, for your advice," Clarence said. "We'll be sure to do what you've told us. And please come back again to give us more facts when you can."

"Oh, I will, I will," he whispered, returning the handshakes. "I just couldn't believe my eyes when I saw you get off the train this morning. 'So now they are picking up *children*,' I thought.'" He shook his head sadly as he put his hat back on. "Where will it all end? Where will it all end?"

He turned and walked to the door. This time, after looking out, he said, "Remember what I've said. Don't eat the meat . . . but follow all the other rules. We'll talk again later."

Then, as if he had an afterthought, he looked over the top of his glasses and added, "You need to be sneaky about the meat, though. Take it on your plate and fool around with it, but throw it away. Whatever you do, don't let them know that you know!"

And with that, he was gone.

CHAPTER 11

After Ronald left, I unrolled the bundle of clothing that Sergeant Lorrie had brought. It was a shirt and a pair of trousers. I went into my compartment and put them on. Since all I had ever worn was dresses, I felt strange when I put the britches on. Both garments were much too big for me. The sleeves completely covered my hands and the trousers covered my feet.

I went back into the sitting area, waving my arms and kicking my feet. I looked like a wild scarecrow, flapping in the wind! We all got a big laugh.

Edward helped me roll up the pant legs and shirtsleeves. We found a thin piece of rope hanging in the tent and tied it around my waist like a belt. It wasn't what I would have liked, but it was better than the heavy velvet dress.

We woke Smokey Joe and the five of us traipsed to the mess hall for lunch. On the way, Scottie told Joe what Ronald Wood had said about not eating the meat. As we entered the dining area, the one thing that was most obvious was the silence. There was no conversation. The men just sat and ate, staring at their food or looking out into space. It was just about the saddest thing I had ever seen in my life.

We spotted Ronald sitting at one of the tables. He just winked at us, and kept eating his food. I saw that there was meat on his plate, but he wasn't eating it. We each got some meat, along with the rest of the food. When we had finished eating, we dumped it in the trash, as Ronald had advised us to do.

After lunch, the boys and Scottie stopped by the tent to get Jiggs. Edward had snuck some bread and cheese in his pocket for the dog to eat. Sergeant Lorrie and Major Andrews were waiting for them by the front gate.

I stood outside the blue tent and watched as they walked across the compound on the way to their audition. It wasn't until I started back inside that it dawned on me. I was here with Smokey Joe—all by myself—for the afternoon. Once again, I recalled the scene in the woods with the wheelbarrow covered in burlap.

We each went to our cubicles to take naps, but, after a while, I got up and sat in one of the chairs in the main room with Maizey in my lap. I was bored. There was nothing to do—no books to read, no paper to write on, no games to play. I wasn't bored for long, however, because Joe, who was apparently feeling better, got up and joined me.

After making rather awkward small talk for a bit, we both began to relax. I found that Joe was good company with a great sense of humor. We talked about the train ride.

"Why is it that you hitch rides on trains if they make you sick at your stomach?" I asked.

"That be a good question, my girl," he answered. "I ask myself that very same question 'most ever' time I jump onto a boxcar." Joe rubbed his whiskers thoughtfully. "But, ye see, while I don't really like trains, I *love* trains. It all goes back a long ways."

"Why don't you tell me about it, Joe? We've got plenty of time."

Joe smiled and nodded his head.

I got up to move to a chair closer to him, and my doll fell to the floor. Quickly, he leaned over and picked her up. He held her gently in his big hands for a moment, touching the doll's face, and smiling pleasantly. He handed her to me.

Then he began his tale. "See, me Pa was a train engineer. Spent his whole life on the railroad. When I was jest a little feller, Pa would take me on runs up and down the tracks." He shook his head and chuckled, "Heh, heh. I felt mighty important when he held me in his lap. I'd be a'settin' there in the front of that train, wearin' his engineer's cap and a'pushin' all kinds o' buttons. Me favorite part, though, was a'pullin' on that big whistle chain. Tooooot, tooooot! I was on top o' the world."

Joe paused again, smiling, lost in his memories. "When I got a bit older, he taught me important things about how t' operate a big steam engine. Sometimes he even let me drive the engine fer a while, all on me own, with him jest a'watchin'. He said I'd grow up to be a engineer someday, too—jest like him. Ah, them was the good ole days."

He leaned back in his chair, staring at the top of the tent with a smile on his lips and a glassy look in his eyes. He sat like that for a long time. Gradually, the smile faded. He looked straight ahead, staring into space. I sat quietly and waited for him to continue.

"One day I was a'playin' out in the yard at our log house. I was makin' little roads in the dirt, pretendin' they was train tracks. I remember it as plain as day. Ma had give me some string and I had tied some sticks together to make 'em into a train.

"I heard a noise about that time, a'comin' down the road. It was a man all dressed in black clothes, a'ridin' on a big black horse. He stopped in front of our place and hitched his horse up to a tree. As he walked past me, he stopped and looked down at me with a sad kind of look. I'll never fergit how tall he looked, a'standin' there on the dirt path. I looked at his black shoes, his black pants and coat . . . all the way up to the black hat that perched up on top of his skinny head.

"He walked on up to the house and knocked on the front door. When Ma come to the door, he told her that Pa was dead. Killed in a train wreck. Pa was gone. Jist like that." Joe snapped his fingers softly. "He never come home agin."

Joe's chin worked up and down as he fought to keep from crying. But he couldn't stop the great tears that filled his eyes and rolled down his grizzly cheeks.

"Ma never got over Pa's death. All the rest of her life, she never seemed happy again. When she passed away, years later, I took to the railroad. Never found another person to take Pa's place in me own life, neither. Guess mebbe I'm jist a good-for-nothing bloke, still a'lookin' fer that." Once again, he stroked his chin and dabbed the tears from his eyes with his dirty handkerchief.

His sad story reminded me a lot of the one we had heard earlier from Scottie. How many of the people in this camp, I wondered, had unlucky stories of one kind or another in their backgrounds? Had most of them become homeless because of circumstances not in their control? Because of something that had happened in their lives? For strokes of bad luck they had experienced?

For the second time that day, I found myself reassuring an adult that sometimes we don't understand why things happen as they do.

"Joe," I said softly, "anybody who is a good-for-nothing bloke would never rescue a kitten off the railroad tracks, the way you did when you saved Maggie's life one day. Only a kind and caring person would do a thing like that."

He nodded in agreement, so I went on. "I've seen you do many chores to help our Mama back at home, like chop wood and hoe the garden. You even helped her pick peas one afternoon not long ago. Why, I've seen you do many acts of kindness around our farm in exchange for a meal." Again he nodded.

I held Maizey out to him. "The gentle way you handed my doll to me, just a few minutes ago, tells me that you are a good-hearted person who cares about people."

Joe looked at me. The twinkle was back in his eye. Talking with Joe in this way made me feel totally at ease with him. I sat back down with Maizey in my lap. I decided that I would dare, once more, to bring up the subject of the digging episode in the woods back home.

"Thanks for sharing your story with me, Joe," I said, "but there *is* something which my brothers and I feel we need an explanation for." I cut my eyes over at him. He gestured for me to continue.

"Edward and I were in our hideout in the woods just before dark yesterday, when we saw you and Scottie there. You were pushing a wheelbarrow filled with something that looked very large. The best we could tell, you buried it there. What was going on? What were you doing?"

"Oh, that." Joe looked at me with a sheepish look on his face. "We didn't know anybody knew anythin' about that. It warn't nothin', really. Hit's jist that we got ourselves in what ye might call a predicament, when . . ."

Just then the door burst open and in came Edward with Jiggs at his heels. Clarence and Scottie were right behind. They were returning from the audition, and were they excited!

"Look what we've got! Look what we've got!" Edward shouted. He held out a bright-colored outfit that looked like a clown suit.

Clarence joined in, enthusiastically. "We really *are* going to be clowns, Emma Mae. Just look at all of this!"

Jiggs was barking his head off. I knelt down to pat him.

"What's that you're saying, Jiggs? Are you telling me that you have a clown suit, too?"

Edward and Clarence laughed. "That's exactly what he's saying, Emma Mae," Clarence said. "Show her, Edward."

Edward held up a bright colored ruffle and a little pointed hat. He put the ruffle around Jigg's neck. The hat had a rubber cord that went under his chin. Then he put on his own hat.

"He looks adorable. It makes him look like he's smiling." Jiggs continued to bark as he jumped around the tent in his costume. He climbed up in Ed's lap. "You make a great pair," I said with a smile.

"What about you, Scottie?" Smokey Joe asked his friend. "Are you goin' to be a clown, too?"

"Be gorrry! I'm to be the jugglin' clown in the show, I am. Got me costume, here, complete with fake noses and makeup for the lot of us."

Just as the three clowns and the dog were calming down from their excitement, the dinner bell began to ring. They put their costumes in their cubicles, and we all went to eat. As before, Edward stuffed some food in his pocket for his little dog's supper.

Since we had been awake such long hours the night before, all six of us, including Jiggs, went to bed as soon as we got back to our tent. We didn't even wait up to hear the bugler play Taps. Thus ended the first day in our strange, new world.

CHAPTER 12

It seemed as though we had barely closed our eyes when we heard the bugle blare—this time playing the wake-up signal called Reveille. We dragged ourselves out of bed, then hurried to the mess hall for breakfast. We skipped the meat, and ate eggs, bread, and honey. The four clowns, including Jiggs, were anxious to get off for their first day's work of being clowns.

Joe and I stayed behind to report for duty. My first assignment for the day was washing dishes. Since I had done that plenty of times at home, I didn't mind; but I had never washed dishes for more than a hundred people before! I thought my back would break!

After that, I was to help put away the fresh milk products and eggs that would be brought from one of the local dairy farms. To my pleasant surprise, the person who came in carrying those supplies was the girl I had seen leaving the complex the day before, when we had just arrived.

We stared at each other in amazement for several moments. It was almost like looking into a mirror, because our facial features were so much the same. I knew my nose was a bit more prominent, and I could see that her chin jutted out at a slightly different angle, but our eyes were the same color, as well as our hair.

"Hello," she said, finally. "My name is Anna."

"I'm pleased to meet you, Anna. I am Emma Mae."

Neither of us knew quite what to say. There was a moment of awkward silence.

Then she said quietly, "I have to admit, I'm a little surprised to see a girl like you in a place like this. How did you come to be here?"

I knew I couldn't go into all the strange details now. Not only was a cranky older man supervising me, but Major Andrews was sitting on the opposite side of the big tent, sipping coffee and chewing on a cigar. He frequently cut his eyes around and glanced at me. It was almost as though he were afraid I might disappear into thin air, or bolt away from the tent. When he looked in my direction, his half-closed eyes gave me the creeps.

I answered Anna's question in a low voice. "It's a very long and quite unbelievable story. I'd love to share it with you sometime, but I'm afraid this is not the time or place."

"Where, then? And when?" she asked.

HOLD SHELF SLIP
Donelson Branch

Customer #: 9112

Item Number: 35192045228537
Title: The tracks /
Placed on Hold Shelf: 5/18/2018

HOLD FOR:

Reed Natalie Ren

Pull Date: 5/26/2018

"I don't have the slightest idea. I've been told that there is no way I can ever leave the premises. I would love to talk with you, though, and get to know you. Do you have any ideas about how we might do that?"

"Excuse me, missy!" interrupted the stern voice of my supervisor. "You need to quit dawdling and put the butter and eggs away now!"

"Yes, sir," I replied. "Right away, sir."

I took the basket of eggs from Anna and began placing the eggs in the container where they were to be stored.

Anna said, "I do have some ideas, but I'll have to check them out. I come to this tent every morning with supplies, so I'll be back again tomorrow."

She handed me the bag of cheese and butter and I gave her the empty egg basket.

"I'll be anxious to hear what you have to say," I responded. I walked with her to the door of the mess hall to get the bucket of milk.

"Until tomorrow, then," she whispered. Instinctively, we each reached out to touch the other's arm. Our mannerisms were exactly the same. We smiled again as she turned and walked away. I stood for a moment, gazing after her. She even walked like me. How could two people who had never even met be so alike? I wondered.

As I went back to my post at the dishwashing sink, I noticed that Major Andrews had stood up to look out the window. He was obviously watching Anna as she hurried across the complex to the main gate. When he looked back in my direction, I quickly turned away, but not before I saw the frown and puzzled look on his face.

Late that afternoon, when the clowns came back from work, they were exhausted. All of them flopped down as soon as they walked in the door.

"You're not as excited as you were when you came back yesterday," I observed.

"That's because we had to work all day. My feet are just about danced out!" Clarence groaned, kicking off his floppy shoes.

"And my lips are just about harmonica-ed out," Edward said. He looked across at me with his brow puckered. "Is that a word, Emma Mae?"

I laughed at him. "*Nein.* Not really, but I get your point. And how about you, little Jiggs?" I reached down and patted the dog that lay with his chin on his front paws. "Did they work you too hard, too?"

Jiggs just blinked his eyes. He didn't even say "Arf."

Scottie shook his head. "Neverrr knew working up a jugglin' act could mean so much prrractice."

They had barely started to relax when the bell began to ring, calling us to eat. After supper, we sat around the lantern-lit room and talked some more about the day.

"Today, Joe and I got introduced to life behind the scene as members of the kitchen patrol. Right, Joe?"

"Uuumph," Joe grunted, shaking his head.

"Not only did I learn all about KP" I went on, "but I had another interesting experience. Did any of you happen to see the girl who was leaving through the gate when we got here yesterday?"

"You mean the one who looked a lot like you?" Edward asked. "I meant to say somethin' about that, but forgot."

"That's the one." I nodded my head. "It turns out, she's the person who brings the dairy supplies to the mess hall every day. Today she brought milk, butter, cheese, and eggs. We look so much alike, we're practically like twins. But here's the spooky part. We also *act* alike."

Clarence asked, "What do you mean, you act alike?"

"She walks like me, and she moves her hands the same way I do. It's kind of like looking at myself in the mirror—until she opens her mouth."

"And what's *that* s'posed to mean?" asked Edward

"She talks funny."

"You mean funny like Scottie?" Edward asked, laughing.

"Not *that* funny," I chuckled. "Just funny. She has a different kind of accent. Anyway, the two of us want to figure out how we can get to know each other. Got any bright ideas?"

"I don't see how prisoners can make plans to meet people from the outside," Clarence said.

"Me, neither," sighed Ed with a shiver. "I *hate* bein' a prisoner."

Just as Edward made that statement, there was a soft rapping at the door. We all jumped.

Clarence went to the door, opened it, and peeped out. Ronald Wood was standing there. He stepped quickly into the tent, once again looking over his shoulder as he entered. Immediately, he closed the door behind him, removing his hat. In his soft voice, he said, "If they catch me in your tent, I'll be sent to prison, just like Major Andrews warned."

"Oh, please, Ronald," I said, "we don't want to get you in any kind of trouble. We appreciate your words of advice and warning, but *please* don't put yourself in danger."

"It's worth the risk," he answered, "if I can prevent you from becoming lifelong prisoners in this place like the rest of us."

"Here, have a seat," Edward said. He moved to sit in the floor by me so Ronald could have a chair. Jiggs climbed in his lap.

"I just wondered if you have any questions about what's happening here that I can help answer," Ronald said.

"Yes," I replied. "We've got plenty of questions. Like, what's really going on here? What kind of outfit is this circus, anyway?"

"Ah, yes," he began. "The circus."

He then launched into a long explanation. "The hobos being held here as captives are the main laborers for this major circus organization. Some of them work as roustabouts, which means they put the circus tents up in the various locations and take them down again when the circus moves to another place. Some are riggers. What they do is "rig" or put up the high ropes for the trapeze and other aerial acts. Others work as animal trainers and keepers."

"And some have to clean up afterr the stinkin' elephants," Scottie moaned. We all laughed at the funny face he made.

Ronald continued. "There are some who are barkers for the side shows, some who do odd jobs, and still others are clowns."

Clarence spoke up, "And, boy, do we know about the clowns!" He reached over and picked up one of the clown noses and stuck it on, over his own nose. Once again, we got a good laugh.

Ronald continued. "Of course, there are other performers who live in another part of the circus community. They're not associated with this complex at all. They're all free to come and go as normal people. I'm sure they are not even aware of how we are being held prisoners."

"I don't understand," I said. "Why do these men all stay here in this complex without rebelling?"

"It's because of the strong system of military organization and enforcement that is being used. More than that, it's the drugs they get in the food. Every last one of these poor souls is being drugged and, therefore, manipulated or controlled . . . and they don't even know it." He shook his head sadly.

"Is there anything that can be done about it?" Clarence asked.

Ronald shook his head again. "I've asked myself that question a million times. I'd give anything in the world if I could help these unlucky people, or if, I, myself, could get back home to my family. I can think of no way it can be done."

"How long have you been here, Mr. Ronald?" Edward asked.

"About two months or so. It's hard to keep track of time here," he answered. "One night I was on my way home from a program at the school where I taught. I always walked the rails, going to and from school. It was late when I walked home that night. I felt good about how things were going in my life, both at school and at home. Then, from out of nowhere, this mysterious train came speeding along in the darkness. The next thing I knew, the train had swooped me up and carried me away. I'm sure my family and the entire community are still looking for my body, which they will never find."

His chin began to quiver, and tears came into his eyes. "I want to go home more than anything in the world," he said. "Perhaps we can work together to find a way to get home."

Just then the bugler began playing Taps. "Oh, I've got to get back to my tent. They check every night to be sure we're all in our beds." He put his hat on as he hurried to the door. "I must go quickly, my friends, but I'll be back soon. Good night."

"*Gute Nacht*," the three of us said in unison.

"*Danke*, Ronald," I added.

He smiled again and waved at us. Then he was gone.

"Well," Clarence sighed after the door shut. "We've got a major project on our hands here. He's not the only one who wants to go home."

Not long after he left, there was another rap at the door. This time it was the guard, sticking his head in. When he saw the lantern light and the five of us sitting around, he glared at us and said, "All right! Lights out! Off to bed! All of you!"

With that, he slammed the door shut. "NOW!" he shouted, as he stomped away.

CHAPTER 13

After breakfast the next morning, our clowns went to meet the guard who escorted them to their place of work. Smokey Joe and I took our places in the mess hall. Once again, Major Andrews lingered after everybody else had gone, but, today, Sergeant Lorrie joined him. They talked in low voices with their heads bent toward each other. I couldn't help but notice, out of the corner of my eye, that, occasionally, one of them glanced in my direction.

Smokey Joe assisted the cook, and I worked the clean-up and odd jobs, as I had done the day before. I hadn't been working long, when I saw Anna coming through the door. Once again she was carrying the large egg basket and a bag.

When she saw me, her face lit up with a smile. I hurried over to meet her. After we exchanged greetings, she handed me the basket, whispering, "After you move all my eggs into your container, lift the towel in the bottom of the basket. There's something I want you to see." She put her hand on my arm. "But don't act surprised when you see it," she warned.

Puzzled, I did what she said. I emptied the egg basket, then I lifted the towel. I couldn't believe my eyes! For there, smiling up at me with her fixed smile, staring eyes, and blond hair was my China doll, Maizey!

My eyes grew wide with surprise. I glanced at Anna. She smiled at me, and winked. I didn't say anything out loud, but my thoughts were racing. This couldn't be Maizey, because I had just kissed her goodbye and laid her on my cot back in the blue tent a short time ago. Could Anna have slipped into my tent, picked her up, then put the towel and eggs on top of her? That wasn't possible.

I looked in the basket again. Wait a minute, I thought. There is something a bit different about this doll. Why, Maizey's dress has blue ribbon trim on it. This doll's dress is exactly the same except that it has a pink trim . . . so this isn't Maizey, after all. Instead, it's a doll that looks identical, except for the color of the trim on her dress.

Anna was patiently standing there, looking nonchalantly around the area. She was giving me time to figure out what the significance of this might be. Finally, I put the towel back over the doll and handed her the basket. As I did so, I whispered, "Where did you get her?"

When I asked, she reached into her apron pocket and pulled out some folded papers. As she took the basket from my hand, she handed the papers to me. I took them, and stuffed them into the pocket of my trousers.

She reached to hand me the bag of cheese and butter, whispering, "Read the message carefully. I'll be back tomorrow." She picked up the egg basket and smiled as she turned and walked away.

I looked to see if the two men who had been watching us were still there, but saw empty spaces at their table. They were gone.

The rest of the day seemed to last forever. When Joe and I finally got off duty, I rushed to the tent to read my letter. Across the top of the page she had drawn a design of ivy and flowers. Below that was the message, written in perfect handwriting. It read:

"Dear Emma Mae,

"When I first saw you walk through the gate carrying your doll, I was amazed. You looked so much like me, and the doll was so like mine, it all seemed very strange.

"Then, after meeting you in person today, I felt even more strange. I told my mother about you and the two boys I had seen with you. She seemed to be interested, but when I told her your name, her mouth flew open.

"'Emma Mae?' she asked. 'What an unusual name for a girl. My sister in Kentucky has a daughter named Emma Mae. She is about your age, Anna.'

"My mother and I started figuring out other things, like the twin dolls. Where did you get your doll, Emma Mae? My Aunt Minnie in Kentucky sent mine to me for Christmas last year."

When I read that part, my heart skipped a beat, for my Aunt Minnie, who is one of my mother's sisters and who lives near me, had given me *my* doll for Christmas last year! I vaguely remembered hearing her say that she was sending another doll to her other niece in Wisconsin. Since I hadn't known that person, I had put the thought out of my mind.

The note suggested that I write a reply, giving as much information about myself as I could. Some blank paper and a stub of a pencil had been stuck inside the note, so I began writing a response, confirming the information about the doll and our family connection.

I could hardly wait for the boys and Scottie to return from work. When they came in, however, they were very tired. They reported that the people had loved their performance. They had gotten wonderful applause and a lot of praise. That was the good part.

The bad part was, between shows, all three of them were required to follow through on Scottie's first assignment. They had to clean the elephants' stalls. They even had to give the large animals their baths. At first, being so close to real elephants had seemed like fun, but after several hours of work, it was no longer fun. It was just that. WORK!

When they finished giving the details about their day, Clarence said, "Changing the subject, but we found out something interesting today. You'll never guess what it is."

"If I can't guess, then why don't you just tell me."

Edward butted in, "Sergeant Lorrie is the ringmaster."

"The what?"

"The ringmaster." Edward and Clarence said together.

"You know how he wears that black top hat and fancy cutaway coat all the time?" Clarence added. "That's because he introduces all the acts. He's the ringmaster for the circus!"

"Why am I not surprised? He and Major Andrews seem to be running the whole show, don't they?" I commented, shaking my head at this new information.

The others nodded in agreement.

"Now it's my turn to share some news," I said.

In a matter of minutes, I told them about the unbelievable coincidence of having some of our own family members right here in this vicinity. Together they read the note that Anna had given me. They were as shocked as I had been.

After we talked awhile, Edward took Jiggs out for some exercise. He was only gone a short time, but when he came back he was excited. In exploring around the tent area, he had spotted a place behind the mess hall where there was a hole in the wall. Just a little hole, he said, but large enough to give him hope for escape.

Apparently none of the guards questioned a little boy out walking his dog. Little could they know that a mere child was beginning to work on a plan that might allow for our escape from captivity.

We went to bed that night with smiles on our faces, but also with a feeling of uneasiness. While the idea of possibly gaining freedom was beginning to form in our minds, we also knew we could be in very great danger. We felt sure these people were keeping an eye on us. And, from what we had been told, we felt even more sure that they did not play games. They played for keeps.

CHAPTER 14

The next morning we were up early, working on a plan to give to Anna. Later, when she came into the mess hall, I slipped her our note with the plan we had dreamed up. She left the tent to read the message. When she returned a few minutes later, she waved at me from the door, nodding her head in agreement.

The remainder of the day went without incident. We were all caught up in getting acquainted with our new situation and way of life.

I awoke the following morning with a rush of excitement. This was the day for us to carry out our plan. I hopped out of bed and carefully braided my dark brown hair into one long braid down my back before I reported for work.

When Anna came in to bring the daily supplies, I saw that her dark brown hair was also braided in one long braid down her back. We smiled at each other and nodded. I was relieved that Major Andrews had not lingered behind today.

After I finished putting the eggs and other supplies away, Anna walked out the front door, as usual, with her empty basket. Then, when nobody was paying attention, I slipped through the flap at the back of the tent.

There was Anna, waiting for me in the bunch of low-growing trees that Edward had noticed behind the mess hall during one of his explorations. We giggled as we quickly took off our outer garments and exchanged them. After we were dressed in the other's clothes, we grabbed each other's hands, laughing softly. Then we shared information that would be important for the other to know. I warned her to be on the lookout for the man in the brown suit and black derby hat, just in case he came lurking around. She told me where to meet her parents outside the gate.

She slipped back through the flap in the tent where she was to resume my job of washing dishes. Joe had been alerted to the switch, so I knew he would help guide her in the rest of her chores.

As Anna disappeared through the flap in the tent, I picked up the empty egg basket. and strolled, nonchalantly, back around the tent, across the complex, past the guards, and out the gate. They never even gave me a second look.

When I got past the gate, I looked to my right. There, beneath a tree, stood a pleasant-looking couple. The woman waved a handkerchief at me, our signal that she was the person I was looking for—but I would have recognized her anywhere as my mother's sister. The family resemblance was very strong.

I ran into their arms. All three of us cried with joy as we exchanged hugs and kisses.

We walked a short distance until we came to their pretty farm wagon. It was painted green with gold stripes. Two beautiful bay horses were tethered to a tree, patiently waiting for the passengers to return.

"Watch your step, my dear," Uncle Cliff said in his clipped accent. "We'll have you out to the house in two shakes of a lamb's tail." Even though what he said reminded me of Papa, his accent sounded even funnier than Anna's.

As I climbed up onto the bench seat beside my Aunt Mary, she put her arm around my shoulders and asked, "Now, where shall we begin?" And that was the starting point of a wonderful new relationship.

After riding for a distance into the countryside, Uncle Cliff tugged on the reins, guiding the horses to turn off the main road into a long tree-lined lane. I could see the large frame house with a wrap-around porch. There was a circular drive in front. Red geraniums and other flowers splashed color into the bright sunlit morning.

"Is this where you live?" I asked my aunt. "Why, it looks like a mansion compared to our place."

"Yes, this is our home. It's not all that grand. Just a good place to raise a large family."

A big red barn with two silos sat on a grassy hillside near the house. The pungent odor of livestock filled the air. A few red apples still clung to the trees in the yard, and the fall colors topped every tree on the horizon. I felt like I was in the middle of a picture postcard or a jigsaw puzzle.

When we pulled up in front of the house, an outburst of noise came barreling out onto the porch and down the steps. It was Anna's three brothers and little sister. Aunt Mary smiled. "Children, can you introduce yourselves to your cousin, Emma Mae?"

The four of them lined up like stair steps. The tallest one said, "I'm Matthew."

The next one said, "I'm Mark."

Then, "I'm Luke."

At the end of the row there stood a cute little girl with dark curly hair and a big, snaggle-toothed smile. "My family ran out of boys, so they had to name me Johnna. My whole name is Johnna Mae, kind of like your name."

"We let the children stay home from school today just so they could meet their cousin from Kentucky." Aunt Mary said.

It turned out to be a wonderful time for getting acquainted and sharing stories. I kept wishing I had the rest of my family to share in it, especially Mama.

The next morning, after breakfast at the farmhouse, I braided my hair down my back again. When the time came, I carried the supplies through the gate and across to the mess hall, just as Anna would normally do. When I saw her doing her duties on the kitchen patrol, I smiled. She looked so much like me, it was like I was seeing myself at work.

As I approached, she glanced up and smiled. We proceeded to go through the daily routine. She accepted the eggs and other products before the two of us slipped out behind the tent and made the same changes we had made the day before, but in reverse order. She left, waving goodbye as she walked away.

Even though Major Andrews was back at his usual place today, more or less watching my actions, we had managed to make the switch behind the building without his being aware of it. I was quite happy about outsmarting him.

Later in the day, when the boys returned from work, we shared our experiences.

"We had a great time getting to know Anna. It's the strangest thing, Emma Mae, how much she looks and acts like you," Edward said.

Clarence added, "At times I could almost forget it was somebody else and not you sitting there."

"Except with her Wisconsin accent she *did* talk kinda funny," Edward chimed in, laughing.

"My trip to visit our aunt and uncle at their farm was wonderful, too," I exclaimed. "We've just got to find a way for you boys to get out there to meet the family and see what a beautiful place they have. They are all as excited about this as we are."

We sat in silence for a bit, thinking about the situation. When the supper bell sounded, we stepped out of our tent and started walking toward the mess hall. We had only taken a few steps, however, when we saw activity on the opposite side of the compound. There were loud voices. A guard had just been summoned to come to that area where Sergeant Lorrie and Major Andrews stood looking at a young hobo who was down on his knees in front of them. The guard's rifle was aimed at the man.

"He's been disrespectful to me for days, now," Sergeant Lorrie said loudly, as he looked at the major. "It seems that he doesn't approve of his job assignment. Thinks he needs a promotion."

"Promotion, huh?" Major Andrews joined in. "The only people who get promotions around here are the ones who die. They get promoted right on out to the county cemetery."

Although we kept walking slowly and acting as though we weren't watching, we couldn't help hearing the loud voices.

The man who was in trouble said, "But I just wanted a chance to work with the big cats. I've always had a talent for training animals and I thought . . . "

"Never mind what *you* thought," the sergeant shouted. "It's what *we* think that counts!"

"That is totally correct," Major Andrews added. "And *we* think you belong in yonder prison." He pointed to the castle-like building. "Guard," he said, turning to look at the uniformed man with his gun, "you know what to do. Take him away! "

The guard moved behind the hobo, who had begun to cry, and poked the gun barrel in his back. "March!" he shouted to the young man, as he struggled to his feet.

"All I wanted to do was help make the show better . . . " he tried explaining again.

"To the prison!" Sergeant Lorrie shouted, as the four of them trudged across the courtyard and out the prison gate. They never even glanced in our direction.

By this time, we had stopped walking. So had the rest of the crowd who was going to supper. We watched solemnly as the little group tromped across the short distance to the prison. The hobo and guard disappeared inside the gates. The two officers then turned and went into the big white house. Even in the near-darkness, we could tell they were pleased with themselves.

Needless to say, our suppertime was quite subdued. After we ate, we walked quietly back to the tent, still thinking about the scene we had just witnessed.

As darkness fell over the circle of colorful tents, Edward took Jiggs out for his nightly walk before bedtime. When he came back, he was excited once again.

"Sharin' time," he announced as he plopped down in a chair. Since Scottie and Joe were already snoozing away in their compartments, Clarence and I pulled our chairs up to the table with the lantern.

Edward spoke in a quiet voice. "I told you the other night that I might have found a way out of here." Instinctively, Clarence and I moved in even closer to our younger brother. The flickering flame from the lantern caused shadows to dance on our faces as we leaned together.

In hushed tones, he went on. "While I was out just now, I looked closer at that hole behind that group of trees. I had been hoping it might be a way to the outside, but I wasn't sure until tonight."

We leaned in still closer, barely breathing as Edward continued his whispered account. "It's not a very big openin', but I used my rubber dagger from my Halloween costume to chip away some of the mortar to make it bigger. "It's about . . . this wide . . . and . . . this deep." He held up his hands to demonstrate the size of the hole.

When I saw the small dimensions he was showing us, my heart sank. There is no way we could get through such a small opening. But Edward went on in his excited way. "I know it don't look like a very big hole, but I crawled out through it and back in again with no trouble. So did Jiggs," he added with a laugh.

Both Clarence and I shook our heads slowly. Edward saw the looks of doubt on our faces, so he went on. "I know both of you are a lot taller than me, but you're kinda skinny. I think you can both get through the hole. No problem!"

With Edward's enthusiasm spurring us on, we proceeded to write out our plan before we snuffed the blaze in the lantern. Taps was being played as we each went to our beds, wondering about our situation here, wondering why a person had been sent to prison for no obvious reason, and wondering if Ed's opening to the outside world could be almost within our reach.

CHAPTER 15

The next morning when Anna made the farm delivery, I slipped the note to her as I reached to get the basket of eggs. We were so smooth in our actions that not even Major Andrews, leaning back in his chair with his feet propped on the table, noticed.

That night, after Taps played and the guard acknowledged that we were quietly in our beds, the three of us got up and crept out of the tent, leaving Jiggs and the others sleeping soundly.

"Follow me," Edward whispered as he tiptoed into the darkness behind the tents. When we got to the space behind the mess hall, he led the way to the hole in the wall. He quickly crawled through the hole, head first.

It was my turn next. Although it was a tight squeeze, I managed to wriggle through to the outside. I was glad, for once, to be wearing men's trousers!

Then it was Clarence's turn. For some reason, he decided to crawl through the opening, feet first. He got his legs past the hole just fine, but when he tried to get his hips through, he got stuck. Edward and I got so tickled watching his long, skinny legs as they kicked around, we could hardly pull on them. Finally, as we each tugged on a leg, his hips popped through, causing us to fall to the ground. Only then was he able to wriggle the rest of his body, his head, and, finally, his long arms through the opening. Ed and I laughed so hard we were almost hysterical . . . until we saw his big dark eyes glaring at us. Our laughter tapered off as we helped him to his feet.

Now that we were on the outside, we looked around. Just as we had hoped, there was a group of people huddled behind some bushes nearby. As we got close, we saw that it was, indeed, our family. There was Aunt Mary, Uncle Cliff, and Anna, along with Matthew, Mark, Luke, and Johnna Mae. They greeted us with warm hugs, kisses, and handshakes.

All ten of us crammed into the large farm wagon, and we were on our way. The horses walked slowly in the darkness, pulling the heavy load into the night. It wasn't long before the horses turned right into the tree-lined lane that led to the big white farmhouse.

"All right," called Aunt Mary when we pulled up to the front steps, "everybody out. Let's gather in the living room so we can talk." Once everybody was situated, she said, "Now, we want to hear more about this unbelievable story of how you three got to Wisconsin on board that mysterious train."

We told them details about the Halloween party and the other events that led up to our finding ourselves on board the nearly invisible wooden train that went screaming through the night. They were speechless after hearing our incredible tale.

Then we talked about the men who live in the circus camp and about the strict rules. We even told them about the nearby prison where rule-breakers are kept. We described the scene we had witnessed just last night. From what we had overheard, there was no reason why the young man had been sent to prison, except he had rubbed one of the leaders the wrong way.

"I've been aware that the circus headquarters are located nearby, of course, since we supply the camp with milk products and eggs," Uncle Cliff said, "but I had no idea most of the men there are hobos and are being held against their wishes. You say they are under the control of two men--one who wears a brown suit and derby hat and the other who wears a black top hat?"

We all nodded.

Uncle Cliff stood up and lit his pipe. He started pacing back and forth, puffing on the pipe. "I've got workers hired to help me finish harvesting my crops here on the farm over the next few days. There is no way I can get away until that's finished." He stopped walking, and leaned down to look us in the eye. "But you can be sure I'll check on all of this as soon as I can. Don't worry, children. I'll start an investigation into this circus operation and find out what can be done about it. And I will do it very soon. Very soon."

"Thanks, Uncle Cliff," Clarence said. "We know you'll do what's right."

Following that, the mood turned to a happy one. We took turns telling stories and sharing about life in both Kentucky and Wisconsin. Even though we seemed to be worlds apart in some ways, we realized that we mostly had a lot in common, especially the appreciation of our families and friends.

The mantle clock in the hall struck eleven o'clock. It was time for us to leave. Aunt Mary, who had grown quiet over the last few minutes, cleared her throat. She said, "I've made a decision. You children will not go back to that dreadful place. We have plenty of room for you to stay right here, where we can take care of you, until we can get you back home to Kentucky."

Without hesitation, Edward spoke up. "I know we've made it sound pretty bad in the camp, but we've just got to go back. We left Jiggs there. Who would take care of that little fella if we didn't return?"

"Ed's right," I agreed. "We'd never think about abandoning Jiggs and our friends. We appreciate your offer, Aunt Mary, but we've really got to go back there for now."

"No," she argued. "I'm putting my foot down. I cannot allow you to put yourself back in that situation, even if it means leaving your dog and friends behind."

"Now, Mary," Uncle Cliff said, "I agree with you that we need to be aware of the danger, but I also see the children's point of view."

Clarence joined the conversation. "Aunt Mary, you sound just like our Mama when you make up your mind about something. I understand that both you and Mama always put the safety of your children first, but, we don't feel really threatened just now."

Anna jumped into the conversation. "Since I come to the camp with supplies every day, maybe we can think of a way for you to give me a warning if there is a new risk or danger."

"What an excellent idea, Anna," Uncle Cliff responded. "If you feel a threat at any point, you can give us the signal and you can be sure we'll be there to help you. What do you think, Mary?"

"I still don't feel good about it," she murmured. "What kind of signal are you thinking about, anyway?"

Clarence said, "Maybe we can put up a special flag somewhere that would get your attention."

"It would have to be something the officers and guards wouldn't notice," I said. "A flag might be spotted by the wrong people."

"I've got an idea," young Edward said, joining the conversation again. "What if we decide on a place where we can put Clarence's red hobo bundle? Like, up on top of the wall behind our blue tent?"

"That's a great idea, Edward," I said. "Then, when Anna brings the supplies to the camp every day, she can look to see if there is a red bundle lying on top of the brick wall."

Anna joined in on the plan. "If the hobo bundle is there, I'll go for help right away. If not, we'll know that everything is still all right inside the camp."

Everybody seemed to like this idea, except Aunt Mary. But even though she still didn't approve of our returning to the encampment, with this new plan in place, she finally gave in.

Before we left, we decided we would follow the same plan to come back to the farm the next night, except we would bring Jiggs with us. Uncle Cliff brought the horses 'round, and we climbed aboard the wagon, ready to be returned to the hole in the wall . . . and our, hopefully, temporary home.

The following night we waited patiently for the time to pass so we could go on our second escapade to the farm. After the playing of Taps, we had the familiar knock on the door. The guard poked his head in, nodded silently when he saw us sitting, huddled around our lantern, then slammed the door shut. Our cabin mates were already asleep.

As soon as he left, I hurried into my compartment. Quickly, I changed clothes. Instead of wearing my usual boy's pants and floppy-sleeved shirt, I had decided to wear the blue velvet dress that had been my Halloween costume. I also put my shoes on. Quickly, I braided my hair and pinned it up on top of my head. As I walked back into the main part of the tent where the lantern glowed, my brothers' eyes grew big in surprise.

"I decided to let them see something more like the real me, instead of the hobo me," I said, smiling. "I'm also taking Maizey, so she can get acquainted with our family tonight." I looked down at the doll in my arms. I thought her painted eyes looked a bit more sparkly than usual. My brothers nodded their approval.

"Okay," I whispered. "I'm ready when you are."

Clarence snuffed out the lantern flame, and we groped our way to the door.

"Have you got Jiggs?" I whispered to Edward as he led the way into the darkness outside.

"Yes," he whispered back. "I've told him our plan, so you can be sure he won't bark."

I smiled in the darkness. Edward and Jiggs were two of a kind!

We followed Ed's lead as we moved stealthily behind the tents until he located the hole in the wall. This time, Clarence went through the hole head first!

As had happened the previous night, the family was there to greet us, gathered behind the cluster of bushes. I was glad to see that Anna had also worn a nice dress-up dress and that she had pinned her hair up, much like I had done. I had whispered the suggestion to her earlier that morning, when she brought the dairy supplies to the black tent. The entire family was happy with our look-alike efforts.

When we got to the farm, we walked up the front steps, as we had done the night before. Just as we passed through the double-front doors, there was a loud shouting of "SURPRISE!" Other family members from the neighborhood had gotten word that Mae and Ed's children from Kentucky were in the area, so they had quickly arranged to have a party in our honor. We had never felt so important in our lives.

A special event of the evening was getting to meet Uncle Cliff's aging parents who were not "long off the boat from Germany," as Aunt Mary put it. We knew that meant they had only recently arrived in Wisconsin from their homeland of Germany.

"They can't even speak American yet," said Johnna Mae, as she sat in the lap of the smiling older woman, who was dressed all in black.

We walked around the house, meeting people and eating the special foods they had prepared. They treated us like royalty—even Jiggs.

"Why, Anna. You and your cousin, Emma Mae, look enough alike you could be twins, especially with your look-alike dolls your Aunt Minnie gave you for Christmas last year." We heard these remarks, again and again, as we strolled with our arms draped around each other's shoulders and our dolls in our arms.

The big event of the evening came when Uncle Cliff asked Edward to play his harmonica. Naturally, when he began to play, Clarence and Jiggs joined in with their dance routine. From the way everybody clapped and carried on, you'd have thought they were the best circus act anywhere in the country.

Time flew by. Before we knew it, it was time to return to our circus jail. Once again, our relatives tried to insist that we stay there, instead of returning to our tent.

"We're not trying to be heroes by going back to the compound," Clarence said, "but we've talked about it together. We all three agree, if we're going to try to help these people, we need to be willing to take a bit of a risk."

Edward and I both nodded in agreement.

I said, "If we ever feel like we're in immediate danger, we'll let you know by putting the hobo bundle on top of the wall, like we decided last night."

Edward, who was holding Jiggs, added, "And, besides, we've really worked hard to get our act ready. We're supposed to headline the show tomorrow. Jiggs would be really disappointed if we didn't get to do it, wouldn't you, fella?"

He moved Jiggs' head up and down to make it look like he was nodding.

Aunt Mary laughed along with the others, but then she shook her finger at us. "If there's the first hint of trouble, you put that bundle out there where we can see it." She hugged each of us tightly. "Now, behave yourselves," she added, sounding exactly like our Mama.

Uncle Cliff loaded us in the wagon and delivered us to the hole in the wall where we crawled through, returning to our captivity. In spite of the wonderful evening we had just experienced with our family, a nagging feeling of fear returned to the pit of my stomach as I tumbled back onto the soft grass inside the encampment walls.

CHAPTER 16

The next day went by much like the days before. The boys' act in the circus had apparently gone well. In spite of that, I could tell, by the looks on their faces when they got back to the tent that afternoon, that something was bothering them.

Joe and Scotty were resting in their cubicles, while the three of us plopped down to relax in the middle room. I looked at my brothers' downtrodden faces. They looked as though they were going to a funeral.

"All right, you two. What's bothering you?" I asked. "I can tell, just by looking at you, that something's wrong. Do you want to keep your secret . . . or would you like to share whatever it is with your big-eared sister who is always glad to listen?"

The boys looked at each other with solemn eyes. Clarence nodded.

Edward began. "Emma Mae, do you remember when Mr. Ronald told us that some people who work in the circus are just regular people and are not hobo prisoners?"

"Of course, I remember. It was on our second night here when he told us how the circus is set up. I think he said that some of the workers and performers are free to come and go, like normal people. Why?"

"There is this other boy we've made friends with, see, who is about our age. His name is Jimmy. We met him on our first day, when we cleaned the elephant stalls."

Clarence joined in. "He's really a nice boy. His parents are the trainers and performers in the horse acts. He's lived around the circus all his life, so this is his home; except their real home is a short distance away, on the other side of the railroad tracks."

Ed continued. "Jimmy's been hangin' around the clown area, watchin' us practice. Most days, he comes to the daytime show so he can watch us perform under the big top."

"What does he do when he's not with you?"

"He works with the horses," Clarence said. "He knows their names and everything about them. He rides them bareback and is learning to do some tricks himself. He'll be able to join his parents in their show before long."

"He sounds like a nice friend. But . . . what's the problem?"

"Jimmy thinks somebody is doing something bad to the horses," Clarence explained.

"Bad? Like hurting them?"

"No, not really causin' them pain," Edward continued. "He just thinks the horses aren't actin' right. And it's not just one or two horses, but all of them. There must be more than a dozen horses in the stalls."

Clarence went on. "The way Jimmy describes it, the horses are acting a lot like the hobos here in our camp. They don't communicate with him any more. They perform their act, and then just stand there."

"That's right," Ed went on. "This afternoon he took us past the other animal cages to the horse barn so we could see them for ourselves. It's true. They just don't look right out of their eyes."

"The poor things," I said. "Why would anybody mistreat an animal like that?" All three of us shook our heads sadly. After a pause, I continued. "I take it that you two have an idea about what might need to be done about all this. Am I right?"

My brothers looked at each other and smiled.

"And I have a sneaky feeling that your sister is somehow going to be involved. Right again?"

They looked at each other again and grinned. "Well, maybe," Edward said, "but we're not sure how it's goin' to work out just yet. That's why we need your help to come up with a plan."

"My first guess is that the problem is most likely food-related. Do you know who feeds the horses? Is it the same person who normally feeds them, or has there been a change?"

"That's the same thing we asked him. This is the part that has us baffled," Clarence explained. "He says he doesn't know. The feeding takes place early in the morning, before they get to the barn, and late in the evening, after they leave. They have never seen the person who actually feeds the horses they work with."

"Why don't they just come right out and ask about the change in their horses' diet?"

"They did that," Clarence said, "and were told that nothing had changed. In spite of that, Jimmy and his family are still convinced that something strange is going on. They have no ideas about who or why, but they're very concerned about the horses, and about their future if the horses keep getting worse."

"So this is where you come in, Sis," Ed smiled.

"Ah, ha! I get to go over there and feed the horses. Right?"

"No, no, no. Not feed the horses. Just sneak around and see who feeds them and find out what it is they give them to eat."

"Do you mean, just go there and watch the horse feedings?"

"Yes, except you have to spy. If there's anything going on that's suspicious, the bad person or persons won't want to be found out," explained Clarence.

Edward continued, "Everybody around the circus durin' the daytime knows us, so we would be recognized if we went there. That's why we need someone who is unknown but who is very clever." He winked at me.

"And who can be sneaky and daring at the same time." Now Clarence winked at me.

"But why me? Surely, with all the other people involved in this huge outfit that makes up the circus, there must be somebody, somewhere, who can get to the heart of this problem and find out what's happening."

Both boys shook their heads. "Jimmy's parents don't think there's anybody they can trust," Edward explained. "The main man in charge of their act in the circus told them that if they think there's a problem with the horses, they can just pack up and leave. He said he has someone else lined up who might take over their show."

Clarence continued, "The thing that makes it so serious is that the family can't just leave, because they don't have anywhere else to go. The circus is their life. Besides, they love the horses and what they do."

Just then the supper bell began to clang. The snoozing sounds in the adjoining rooms stopped abruptly as our cabin mates got ready to walk across to the mess hall with us for our evening meal. Smokey Joe barged out of his cubbyhole. "Anybody else around here hungry besides this ole bum?"

"Sure, Joe," I responded, patting him on the back as he swaggered through the door. Scottie followed him out.

As we started walking toward the mess hall, I looked at my brothers and said, "One more quick question. If I decide to help out, what will my first step be?"

My brothers looked at each other and grinned. "We'll tell you that when we get to the dairy farm tonight." And with that, Edward reached over and hit Clarence on the arm, laughing, as he said, "Got you last!" Then he took off at a run across the open space towards the big black tent, with Clarence giving chase in their favorite game of Tag.

Later that night, we crawled through the hole behind the black tent, to meet our relatives. Once again, the shared time with the family was wonderful, as we talked, laughed, sang, and played.

Before we knew it, the clock on the mantle in the hall chimed eleven o'clock—departure time. We hugged goodbyes to all the cousins and Aunt Mary, telling them that we would see them the next night. Uncle Cliff had helped us up into the spring wagon and gathered up the reins to leave, when Anna came running down the steps with a bundle in her hand. "Emma Mae!" she called. "You're about to forget your *disguise*!"

"Ah, yes. My *disguise*," I laughed. "I can hardly wait to see how I'm going to look dressed like a boy."

Clarence reached down to get the bundle of clothes. "Thanks, Anna, for helping your brothers find the right kind of clothes for Emma Mae."

"Just be careful, my dear, whatever it is you're up to," cautioned Aunt Mary. "A disguise, indeed. Tsk, tsk, tsk!" She shook her head disapprovingly.

"I will, Aunt Mary, I promise. I *think* my role is to be a horse food detective, but I'll have a full report when we see you tomorrow night. Same time? Same place?"

"Yesss," they all chorused, waving goodbye.

"Giddy-up, horses," Uncle Cliff said, giving the horses their signal to move. The three of us waved goodbye to the children and Aunt Mary as they stood on the steps, sending us back to our adventures in the compound.

CHAPTER 17

Reveille seemed to come early the next morning. When I heard the now-familiar sound of the trumpet playing the wake-up tune, it was all I could do to get my eyes open. Somewhere in the back of my brain, there lurked an uneasy feeling that something was about to happen—something that might not turn out well.

"Emma Mae? Are you awake yet?" whispered Clarence from the other side of my cubbyhole flap.

"More or less," I answered, as I stretched and yawned. "I'll get up in a minute."

I looked around in the semi-darkness of my tiny space. What was that piled in the corner of my cubby? Oh, yes. It was the bundle of clothes that we brought with us from the farm last night. I jumped from my cot. Quickly, I donned the long-sleeved white shirt, the brown knicker pants with suspenders, the brown-and-white plaid knee socks, and brown leather shoes. I leaned over so that my long hair dangled down. I bunched it up and pinned it on top of my head with the hairpins that Anna had included. I placed the cap on my head, covering the hair. Looking down at myself, I liked what I saw, so I stepped through the flap into the main room of the tent.

Both brothers were sitting there in the dim light cast off by the lantern, waiting. Their faces lit up enough to brighten the room when they saw the transformation of their sister-turned-boy!

"Do you think I can get past the bad guys dressed like this?" I asked.

"Major Andrews himself wouldn't recognize you in that outfit, Emma Mae! You can get past all the guards, for sure, because they never pay much attention to children over at the circus."

"Even this early, though?" I asked. Now I knew the reason for my earlier feeling of uneasiness. "Why would a child be roaming around behind the scenes of a circus at the break of dawn?"

"That's the question of the hour," Clarence responded, "and that's where your clever little mind will take over. I'm sure you can come up with something."

"You'd better get going, Sis. You have to report for work at the mess hall in about an hour. Do you want us to walk across the camp with you to the circus tent area?"

"*Nein*, Ed, but thanks anyway. I'm afraid three kids out this early might call attention to us. You've told me how to find the horse barn, so I'll be fine on my own."

Instinctively, both boys reached out and clasped my hands, giving them a squeeze. "Be careful," Clarence whispered, as I opened the door and slipped out into the dim light of early morning.

I quickly raced past the big trees in the open space of the compound. Not a person was in sight. When I got to the large gate that led from the camp into the circus premises, I slowed down. The tall wooden gate was closed, as I presumed it would be, but that was no problem to a farm girl who was accustomed to climbing fences and gates back home. In no time at all I found myself on the other side. There was still no one in sight.

I knew that the big top tent, where the circus performances took place, was to my right, because I had snuck into the big tent to watch my brothers' act two days ago.

Now, using the directions the boys had told me, I moved around to the left. This was the area where the animals lived. Being so early, most of them were still sleeping. As I jogged quietly along, I saw cages with all kinds of creatures. The bears were asleep. So were the zebras and llamas. The beautiful big cats, however, had their eyes at half-mast. Those sleepy-looking eyes followed me suspiciously as I walked quickly in front of their cages.

When I got to the elephant stalls, I just had to stop for a minute and take a look. I am always amazed at the size and majesty of these huge animals. My nose told me, though, that my brothers and Scottie had work to do when they checked in later this morning. Ugh! They would have to "clean up after the stinkin' elephants," as Scottie would say.

Next after the elephants, I passed stalls of other animals. Some of them were not familiar to me. When I saw monkey cages with all kinds of monkeys inside I wanted to stop and take a look, but knew I didn't have time. Besides, I could see the horse barn just ahead, so I hurried on.

I was surprised that the large barn was separate from all the other buildings. It had tall double doors that were closed and locked. By now the sky had lightened enough so that I could see quite well. It was obvious there was no way into the barn except by using a key on the rusty-looking lock and chain that held it shut. There was an open hayloft high above, but no ladder magically appeared for me to climb.

I did a quick run around the entire barn to see if there were other openings. The only other entrance was the double-doors at the opposite end, but they, too, were locked with a chain. I stood looking desperately at the tightly secured building in front of me. "Think, Emma Mae, think!" I said to myself. "How can a tall, thin person get inside a barn that is locked at both ends?"

At that precise moment, the sun peeped over the horizon. A shaft of sunlight slanted straight through the surrounding tents and buildings. It looked as though a spotlight had suddenly appeared, lighting up a small area near the lower left corner of the barn. There in the beam of sunlight, I saw—not just one broken barn board—but two of them, right together. They were cracked about four feet above the ground. It was barely noticeable that they were split at all.

I dashed to the spot and pushed hard just below the crack. To my great surprise, the boards jiggled a little. I stood back a couple of steps, then gave the boards a good swift kick, just above the ground. The boards started to give. One more kick was all it took. What luck! The boards swung outward at the top and inward at the bottom, creating a small open space at ground level. It was not a very big opening, since it was just two barn boards wide, but it was enough for a thin girl who was dressed like a boy to wriggle through. When I got inside, I immediately pushed the boards back in place to plug the hole.

So I was inside the barn. Now what?

It took a few seconds for my eyes to adjust to the darkness inside, but it didn't take my ears long to hear the sound of a horse breathing through its lips, with that blubbery kind of sound that horses make. I was actually in a stall with a horse.

Now that I could see, I could tell that it was a very large horse. It was chestnut brown with huge white feet and legs. Its face, too, was white, but its black mane tumbled over its neck and between its ears, creating bangs on its forehead. It was the most beautiful horse I had ever seen in my life. To make things better—or worse—there were two of them. They were both staring straight at me, with a dull look in their eyes.

I knew right away that they were Clydesdale horses. I had seen and admired horses like these in circus parades back in my hometown of Paducah, Kentucky, but I had never had a chance to look at them at close range. My heart was beating like a drum.

Once I calmed myself down, I did a quick appraisal of the situation. The horses stood silently, side by side, facing the outside wall. An empty feeding trough hung on the wall a few feet off the floor. A container of water sat nearby. Hay covered the floor of the stall.

"Hello, Clyde and Dale," I whispered to the horses. I rubbed the velvety soft muzzle of the one closest to me that I thought looked like Clyde. "At least they seem to be taking good care of you, overall." He nodded his head up and down, as if in response to my remark.

I was a bit unsure about moving around to the hind parts of the horses, seeing how huge their feet were, but I knew I had to get out of the stall before the feeding crew arrived. I moved slowly toward the door, whispering, "Nice, horsies. Nice, horsies." They turned their heads with their big, solemn eyes, watching me go.

The sliding wooden bolt on the door was easy to open. I let myself out into the hallway of the barn, before pushing the bolt back into place. Now that I was inside the barn itself, I did a quick look-around. There were stalls all along both sides of the wide, open hallway. It was extremely clean . . . and it didn't even smell like a barn.

In the farthest stall, I saw the head of a giraffe, as it stuck its long neck through the opening above the stall wall. I thought it was a bit odd for a giraffe to be living in a horse barn, but I didn't take time to dwell on it. The giraffe watched me with curious eyes as I made a quick run the length of the hallway and back.

The only place I saw where a spy might hide was in the hayloft, high above the stalls in the building. The ladder to the loft was located in the middle of the barn. In a flash, I climbed the ladder and looked around. It was a most unusual hayloft, but before I had time to investigate it, I heard the barn doors at the opposite end of the barn being unlocked. Sunlight streamed into the huge space as the doors swung open. Then I heard voices.

Relieved that I had gotten out of sight in time, I now began to concentrate on my next move. Somehow I needed to see who the people were, and I needed to see what they were giving the horses to eat.

As luck would have it, the hayloft was built with a large opening all the way down the middle of the barn. A tall, fence-like rail surrounded this open space. The loose hay was piled high, all around the railing. With this arrangement, the hay could easily be tossed over the railing down into the hallway below. It was a wonderful setup for pitching fresh hay down for the animals. It was also convenient for a detective like myself to make peepholes along the way, as the persons below moved from place to place.

From this vantage point, not only could I see them, but I could also hear the conversation of the two people who had entered the barn. It was a middle-aged man and an attractive younger woman. The man had his arm around the woman's shoulders.

"So you had a chance to speak to the circus manager again yesterday, did you? What did he have to say this time about your getting a riding job here at the circus, Erina?" the man asked. He spoke in a rather high-pitched voice.

When she responded, I had to listen especially hard to hear her soft reply. She had an unusual accent that made it even harder to understand.

"He say, once more, that he like to hire me and my brothers to do horse show in circus, but he have no job open now."

"Yes," the man said, "that's what he said before. Since you talked to him last, I've been thinking about how I might help you get that job. You know how much I would like to have you and your brothers right here in the circus near me." He leaned over and kissed her before continuing. "I've already been working on a plan. I mentioned it to you earlier. Do you want to hear more about it?"

"*Da*," she replied. "Yes, one other time you tell me that you have plan."

At this point, the two of them were standing near the middle of the barn. Occasionally, he reached out and stroked her face or patted her shoulder.

"Erina, you know I am an animal doctor. I have all kinds of food as well as medicines that I give to animals when they need them."

"*Da*, that is one reason my brothers and myself like you. In our homeland of Russia, we grow up with many animals."

"That is good. Now, here is the plan I am working on. I am feeding the horses some drugs that make them appear to be tired. They don't respond well anymore."

"I so sorry, Dr. Hess, but I not understand."

"Please, Erina, call me Wendell," he said, smiling at her.

"Okay, Wendell. Tell me more of plan."

He put his hand on her shoulder, and continued. "I have drugs . . . kind of like medicine . . . you know . . . medicine?"

She nodded her head. "*Da*. I know medicine."

"It does not hurt the horses when I give them small amounts, but it does slow them down so that they no longer act in a normal way."

"It does not hurt horses to take medicine?"

"No, but after a short time of getting this drug, day after day, they stop responding in their usual way. They no longer want to prance and dance. They simply want to stand and stare. Do you understand so far?"

"The horses no longer want to do show in circus?"

"Exactly, Erina. They will no longer want to perform in the circus. This means, of course, that the present trainers and performers will not be able to stay on the job. They will have to quit the circus and move to another place."

"I theenk I understand, Wendell. After other people leave circus, then you make horses all better, and my brothers and myself get job."

He laughed quietly. "*Da*. Do you think it will work, sweetheart?"

"It will not hurt ze horses?"

"There is no way I would hurt the horses," the man replied. "After all, I am a veterinarian, an animal doctor. I'm just giving them small amounts of this drug so that it will make them react slower and slower. After the other people quit the show and move away, I'll have my 'special medicine' ready and the horses will return to their normal actions."

The young woman clapped her hands and gave him a kiss. "When ze horses be normal, ze 'Rough-Riding Russians' weel still be around. Then we be hired as best horse riders in country. Theenk it weel work?"

"It's already working. The horses are getting slower every day."

As the last part of this conversation was taking place, the couple was moving between the stalls. The man carried a tow sack filled with oats or other food for the horses. The woman carried a small sack. Outside each stall, he filled a pail with the main food and held it out to her. She dumped in a cup full of whatever it was in her bag. She stirred it in the oats, then she waited while he went in the next stall and, apparently, emptied his bucket. After what I had heard, I assumed the bag she was carrying was the one with the drugs in it, and they were combining the drugs with the regular food.

I had seen and heard enough. I also knew my time was running out. I needed to get back to the blue tent to change clothes, and, after that, go to work in the mess hall. I was peering through an opening in the hay along the rail, plotting on how to get down from the loft without being seen, when it happened.

In my excitement, I had forgotten that I am allergic to hay. Any time I am around hay for a while, I start to sneeze. So it happened that, just as the doctor below was about to enter the stall with Clyde and Dale, I sneezed!

"What was that?" Dr. Hess shouted.

"Ze horse, she sneeze?" asked Erina.

"That wasn't a horse's sneeze!" he yelled. "That was a human sneeze! But . . . who? Where? What?" Obviously, he was extremely upset. He walked briskly up and down the length of the hallway in the middle of the barn. When he got even with the ladder to the hayloft again, he stopped and looked up, turning to view the loft for the first time.

"Here! Hold this bag!" he said loudly. "I'll climb up there and take a look around." He handed her the bag of feed and jumped onto the ladder.

From my vantage point, I watched this latest development in horror. Unless I moved quickly, he would definitely locate me. And I was certain he would not be happy that the recent conversation had been overheard.

I knelt for another second, holding my nose so I wouldn't sneeze again, assessing my situation. No way could I go down the way I had come up, since the ladder was occupied. I couldn't just jump for it.

The loft was much too high, and I could be hurt. There was not a rope nearby that I could swing down on. What to do? What to do?

Dr. Hess was halfway up the ladder by now. I was still hidden behind the hay in the middle of the loft on the opposite side, when a thought hit me like that earlier ray of sunlight.

There was one thing that was tall enough to give me an advantage, and it was at the opposite end of the barn, away from Clyde and Dale. Immediately, I began moving in a hunched over position, still hidden behind the piled up hay.

"Is anybody up here?" Dr. Hess hollered in a rough-sounding voice when he reached the top of the ladder. As if a person would answer that question, I thought as I scurried through the hay toward the far end of the loft. But he continued, "I can hear you over there. You'd better stop and make yourself known!"

"Dr. Hess? Wendell? You okay up there?" came a voice from below. I figured, from the location of her voice, she was still standing near the ladder in the center of the barn. Perfect, I thought.

By now I was at the far end of the barn. I grabbed my nose again, to stifle one more sneeze. Without waiting another second, I jumped through the hay that was piled against the railing. It was easy to climb over the tall rail, then climb down again on the opposite side. And there, just as I had hoped, was the head of a very tall giraffe.

I swung my legs around, looping them around the startled animal's neck. The giraffe made strange snorting sounds as it swung its head back and forth, trying to get rid of this unexpected burden that had suddenly appeared from out of nowhere. In a flash I shimmied down the entire length of its neck, landing on my feet in the straw inside the stall. In the dark corner of the booth, I could make out a baby giraffe sitting on its haunches, but there was no time to stop and look at it.

I gave the mother giraffe a soft pat on her side, whispering, "Thank you, ma'am," as I unlatched the stall door and ran to the large open space in the barn door at the far end of the building.

"Stop! Stop!" I heard Dr. Hess yelling. "Young man! Stop, I say!"

I dared to take one last look. The woman had dropped the feedbags and was standing in the middle of the hall with a hand on either side of her face. Her mouth was open wide, and her blue eyes, filled with alarm. "Nyet!" she cried. "No!"

I laughed softly, complimenting myself for a job well done. I raced around the corner of the barn, ran the length of it, and was headed back past the monkey cages, when, suddenly, the laughter died in my throat. I stopped in my tracks. Someone was strolling straight down the walkway toward me, and it was someone I recognized immediately. It was none other than Major Andrews! He was looking straight at me . . . and he was only a few feet away.

Instinctively, I reached up and pulled the cap down over my forehead as far as I could. While my hand was in front of my face, I used it to cover a fake sneeze. "Excuse me, sir," I said in a deep voice. "I seem to have caught a fresh cold." Then I sneezed again.

I knew it was weak acting, but it was the best thing I could think of under the circumstances. I stepped to the right of the walkway to bypass him.

He stopped abruptly and my heart skipped a beat. "I don't know what you're doing out here so early, young man, but it sounds as if you'd better get back home and take care of that cold." He fiddled with his black derby hat while he was talking. Then, without further ado, he began walking away.

"Thank you, sir, I will," I replied in my phony male voice. I had barely slowed my pace of walking during this interchange. I started walking faster, away from the man in the brown suit. But as I began picking up speed, I turned around to get one last look . . . just in time to see that he, too, had stopped and turned to look in my direction. And to hear him say loudly, "Wait a minute! Don't I know you from somewhere?"

I took off running so fast that the next part of my return trip out of the circus and across the open space of our tent village was like a blur. I never thought I would be so glad to be back in the safety of a blue tent that I shared with my brothers and two homeless men who were possibly killers.

Since they had, obviously, gone to breakfast, I flopped down on my bed to let my heart return to normal. After a minute or two, I changed clothes, putting on my regular work garb. I pushed the borrowed clothing under my cot in case Major Andrews should come checking my room. Only then did I stop to think about the information I had overheard in the barn.

Someone was, indeed, harming the horses. And now they knew that someone else knew. Would Major Andrews figure out the identity of the sick boy he met on the walkway? And, if so, what would he do about it? The familiar question raced through my head: Where would this all end?

CHAPTER 18

As he had done most mornings since we arrived, Major Andrews came to the big tent for coffee. I felt sure his appearance was earlier than usual. Since he looked directly at me as he entered, I was glad I had skipped eating breakfast and gone straight to washing dishes when I arrived. There was no way he could know that I was late getting to work.

Out of the corner of my eye, I saw him watching me, off and on, throughout the morning, shaking his head slowly. He kept a puzzled look on his face.

When Sergeant Lorrie arrived, I had the strange feeling that I was being discussed as the two men dawdled, once again, over their coffee and cigars. To be honest, from the way the two of them watched me, I felt quite uneasy. When I thought about it, though, I couldn't think of anything I had done wrong, other than stomping a certain person's foot in anger several days ago and eavesdropping in a hayloft.

I began to wonder if there might be more to it than that. It seemed strange that two adults would spend time watching a young girl work. Every time I stopped to talk to someone or interact with another person, like when Anna brought the supplies, I noticed their eyes were glued on me.

Then I observed something else. They also seemed to be watching Smokey Joe as he lumbered around in the kitchen. In his good-natured way, he often stopped to chitchat with someone, or to laugh at himself if he made a bumble of some kind, like if he dropped a pot or pan. The puzzled looks on their faces actually puzzled me.

When the clowns came in from work that afternoon, our little group, including Joe and Scottie, sat around the tent to share about our day. I decided to bring up my concern.

"There's something going on that's bothering me," I said. "I feel uneasy about the way the two main men in this operation watch me when I'm at work. I've noticed that they keep a sharp eye on Smokey Joe, too. Do any of you have an idea why?"

"I don't have the foggiest," Clarence said.

"Me, neither," Edward joined in, "but it does seem odd."

"I don't think it's just my imagination. Today was the worst day yet." I sighed. "It's starting to make me nervous. I just wish I knew why."

"I've been a'noticin' it, too," Joe said, "and I got me a theory."

"Wot's that, Joe?" Scottie asked.

"I think we're actin' too bright."

"Wot do you mean, 'too brright?'"

"I mean we ain't actin' like the meat is makin' us into wind-up toys."

"That's it!" I exclaimed. "Why hadn't we thought about that? If we'd been eating the meat like the rest of the crew, we should all be slowing down by now." I jumped up and hugged him. "Smokey Joe, you're my hero!"

Joe just beamed as I planted a kiss on his grizzly, bearded face. "I ain't never been called a hero before," he said. "I ain't never been kissed by a purty young lady before, neither." He actually blushed.

Clarence, who was smiling at this display of affection, said, "So I guess the bottom line is, we need to act dull and lifeless any time we're around the big chiefs."

"The way I feel right now," Edward chimed in, "acting dull and lifeless won't be too hard, 'cause I, for one, am really tired after today's workout."

"That makes two of us, me lad. I think the elephant job just about worre me out this afterrnoon." Scottie stood and stretched. Then he said, "I'm going to get a bit of a rrest before supper, if ye don't mind."

"Guess that makes three of us," Joe said. "I'm goin' to me room and practice bein' dull and lifeless fer a bit, meself." We all laughed as he, too, stood and left the room.

Now that my brothers and I were alone, I gave them a brief account of what had happened on my expedition to the horse barn that morning. I promised I'd give full details when we met with the family later that night.

When the supper bell rang, we made our way to the mess hall, laughing among ourselves as we practiced our dull and lifeless expressions. We were sorry our two leaders weren't there to see our performance.

After Taps, we made our regular exit through our now-familiar hole in the wall, and rode off into the night with our Wisconsin family. Since the weather had turned cooler, the whole family gathered around the fireplace in the large living room to keep warm. Uncle Cliff lit his pipe, as usual, and leaned against the mantle.

Everybody was anxious to hear the full report on what had happened with the horse-spying episode that morning.

I told them about the events that took place, giving all the details I could recall. When I got to the part describing how I overheard the doctor and young woman discussing the scheme and mentioned Dr. Hess's name, both Uncle Cliff and Aunt Mary gasped. They looked at each other in alarm.

"What?" I asked. "Did I do something wrong?"

"No, no, no. It's not you, dear," Aunt Mary responded. "It's just that a Dr. Hess is the veterinarian who takes care of our cattle and other livestock. We consider him to be a good friend."

"What did he look like?" asked Uncle Cliff. "How did he sound?"

"I couldn't get a perfect look at him since I was looking down from above, but his hair was reddish-colored, and I could tell that he was balding on top. He had a kind of high-pitched voice."

"Oh, dear. Oh, dear," Aunt Mary said softly. "That describes our Dr. Hess 'to a T'. What about the young lady? You said she talked with an unusual accent? What was she like?"

"She was very pretty. She had long blond hair. She seemed nervous about putting the stuff in the horses' food until he explained that it wouldn't hurt the horses. It would just make them lazy and dull. He also told her that when the present horse trainers were fired, then she and her brothers would get the job."

"Cliff," Aunt Mary said, "do you remember that two young men came here a few weeks ago, looking for work? They were asking about the horses. Do you think they could be related to this girl?"

"Hmmm." He puffed on his pipe. "Now that you mention it, I recall that they spoke with a strong accent. Actually, I believe they said Dr. Hess had sent them our way."

"Emma Mae, did they mention any other names during the conversation?" Aunt Mary asked.

"Yes, he called her . . . ummm . . . Erina, I think. Something like that. And she called him Wendell."

"Well, for goodness sake, then it *is* our veterinarian. Dr. Wendell Hess. Oh, dear. Oh, dear." She covered her mouth with a handkerchief, just the way Mama does when she's worried. Both she and Uncle Cliff sat staring at the fire with deep furrows on their foreheads.

We all sat quietly for a minute, thinking about the information that was being discussed. Even the younger children were still.

Clarence broke the silence. "From what I'm hearing, this Dr. Hess is not doing the horses any real harm. It sounds like he's controlling how they act so his girlfriend and her brothers can get a job. Is that what you think, Uncle Cliff?"

"That's how it sounds to me."

"I'm beginning to think of something that might help the situation," Aunt Mary said, thoughtfully.

"What's that, my dear?"

"Since your parents recently came here from Germany, Cliff, and are staying with your sister, she told me, just today, that she could use an extra pair of hands to help with housework. Do you think she might be interested in offering this young woman a job?"

"That's an excellent idea, Mary. Along that same line, our neighbors up the road have let it be known they are looking for dependable workers to help take care of their livestock. They especially need help with the horses they board over there. That might be a good opportunity for these young men."

Clarence jumped into the conversation. "I just hope the horses get back to normal in time for Jimmy's family to keep the show going over the winter."

Edward said, "By the time the circus comes back from winter break, they might want to have two horse acts instead of one. Then everybody can live happily ever after."

Uncle Cliff chuckled. "Not a bad idea, my boy. Not a bad idea. But you say it's already time for some of the workers to go away for the winter?"

"Yes, that's what Ronald Wood told us this morning," Clarence explained. "He said the people who live here in Racine will continue the show through the winter, but on a smaller scale."

"Well, then. I'm going to write a note to Dr. Hess for Emma Mae to deliver to the barn early tomorrow morning." He looked at me and sighed. There was a deep furrow between his brows, showing that he was thinking hard. The glow in his pipe glared red. "It will not have my name signed to it, but it will let him know that there are certain people who are aware of what's going on with the horses."

"This means I get to wear my boy disguise again?" I asked with a slight shiver.

"I think so, my dear. Just to deliver the message . . . that's all. No spying or snooping this time. Just tack the message to the door early in the morning."

Anna, who had been sitting near me on the floor, quietly listening to the conversation, said, "I'm glad you got that all worked out. Now, Emma Mae, maybe you can tell us the rest of the story about how you got out of that hayloft this morning. We've all been waiting to hear. What happened next? Weren't you scared half to death?"

The other children joined in, anxious to hear how the story ended. I took up where I had left off earlier. There was a lot of laughter as I acted out my sneezing episode. I demonstrated how I had jumped onto the giraffe's neck, swooshed down, then left the barn before the others knew what had happened. Then I showed them how I had talked when I met Major Andrews on the walkway. The family applauded me as I re-enacted the events. Once again, the evening ended on a happy note.

When we left their home a short time later, I had a neatly written note tucked into the pocket of my hobo trousers, ready to be delivered to the barn the next morning. But I also had an uneasy feeling about the task that lay ahead of me, come the dawn.

CHAPTER 19

The day broke, bright and clear. When I first woke up, I went to the front door and peered out. The cloudless blue sky told me it was going to be one of those gorgeous days that only takes place in early November. Colorful leaves drifted from the trees around our complex. I took all of this as a good sign.

I went back to my cubby. My next actions were a duplicate of yesterday—I put on my boyish attire, sprinted across the open field, climbed the fence, darted past the animal cages, and stopped to look up at the looming horse barn.

The broken barn boards in the corner, where I had crawled into the stall with the horses yesterday, looked practically normal. I could hardly tell they had ever been moved. I scurried along the left-hand side of the barn.

When I got to the far end, which is where Dr. Hess had entered the day before, I stopped and looked around. Not a person was in sight. The large doors were still locked with the padlock. As I took the note and envelope from my pocket, I glanced at the message one more time. It was printed in bold letters:

> **"Certain people in connection with the circus are aware of your ill treatment of the horses. You must let the horses get back to their normal lifestyles at once!"**

I refolded the note and stuffed it in the envelope that Uncle Cliff had given me. I took the hammer and two nails and tacked the envelope to the door, just above the padlock. I re-read the words printed on the envelope: "**ESPECIALLY FOR DR. WENDELL HESS!**" I nodded my head sharply to emphasize the exclamation point at the end, and walked back around the barn.

Since my mission was accomplished and there was still nobody in sight, I decided to follow through on my secret desire to see Clyde and Dale once more. I stopped at the corner where the loose barn boards were located. I gave the boards a couple of swift kicks, and, as they had done yesterday, they flipped out from the top and in at the bottom. I turned my body sideways so I could squeeze through the tiny space again, headfirst.

The scene inside looked exactly the way it had the day before. Both horses looked at me with glum eyes. Their mouths were turned down at the corners, giving them a sad appearance. Realizing that I didn't have much time, I reached in my other pocket and pulled out the apple I had picked off the apple tree at Aunt Mary's house last night before we left. I had cut the apple into wedges and wrapped them in a piece of newspaper.

Now I moved to stand between the two horses, with the apple slices in my outstretched hands. How special it was to be petting such magnificent animals, and to feel the velvety muzzles and soft tongues as they ate the fruit. When they finished, I stroked their beautiful white faces for several minutes, before I gave each of them a kiss on their long noses. "Goodbye, Clyde. Goodbye, Dale," I whispered as I turned to leave. I thought they looked a notch happier as I crawled back through the opening to the outside and pushed the boards back in place.

Since there was still nobody in sight, I gave in to my curiosity and watched the monkeys for a bit. It was great fun to see them swinging around on the limbs and rope swings inside their cages. I gave them silent applause as I moved away.

To my relief, the return trip to the blue tent was without incident. I got there just in time to switch to my regular hobo clothes and go to breakfast with our group. We put on our dull and lifeless expressions. There was no talking during the entire meal. Joe and I both continued the act as we began our routine work in the kitchen in the big black tent, especially while the boss men were around.

That night we sat around our table after our tent mates had gone to sleep, waiting for the routine guard check.

"After what Ronald Wood said today, it sounds like tonight might be our last visit with our Wisconsin family," Clarence said glumly. "He's pretty sure the entire group will be shipping out on the train, headed for Florida, on the day after tomorrow."

"At least, we'll be out of this prison camp," Edward said quietly.

I looked at my brothers as they sat across from me. "But who knows what that might mean? From the way Major Andrews glared at me today, it might mean that I'll simply be transferred from prison camp to *prison*." I shuddered.

"One thing's for sure," Clarence continued, "we've got a lot of work to do if we're going to come up with a plan of action that will set these hobos free."

Just as he said that, there was a quiet rapping on the door. The door opened slowly. For a long minute, the regular guard stood there, gazing suspiciously at first one of us and then another. He raised his left eyebrow and smiled a smile that only turned up one side of his mouth. "Lights out," he said, closing the door softly as he left.

The three of us looked at each other with big eyes. "That was too weird," I whispered. "He's never done anything like that before."

"Do you think he might have been outside listening to us?" Clarence asked softly.

Edward responded, "I just got another case of the heebie-jeebies. What do you think he'll do if he heard us?"

"I guess we'll find out, sooner or later," I said quietly as I stood up. Maizey was in my lap. I wanted her to go with me to see our family for the last time. "I'm sure the family is waiting for us, though, so we'd better get going. I'm just sorry our visits have to end."

Clarence, standing and stretching, said, "Just because it's our last visit to their house doesn't mean this all has to end." He picked up the lantern and started lowering the flame.

Edward stood, too, holding his sleeping dog in his arms. "I know for sure that Mama and Aunt Mary write letters. We can always do that."

"You're both right, of course," I agreed. "Come on. Let's go."

Clarence extinguished the lantern light. We groped our way through the darkness to the doorway and out into the pitch-black night. This time I led the way as we crept away from our tent. Suddenly, as my eyes adjusted to the darkness, I had the distinct feeling that I saw movement somewhere around the trees in the middle of the complex. Since I was in the lead, I stopped short, staring in that direction. Both boys bumped into me.

"What the . . .?" Clarence whispered.

"Did you see something moving out there?" I asked.

"Out where, Emma Mae?" Edward's voice sounded cross.

"By the trees in the middle."

"Why would there be anything moving at this time of night, for crying out loud?" Clarence muttered.

"Why would Major Andrews watch all of us so closely all the time?" I responded. "I don't know. Now I guess *I've* got the heebie-jeebies."

We stood still for a moment longer as we peered through the darkness toward the clump of trees. Seeing nothing move, I sighed. "It was probably my imagination. Sorry, boys. Let's go."

When we crawled through our hole that was getting bigger with each passing night, our family was waiting for us. For the first time since we had started meeting like this, our ride through the dark, chilly night was quiet. Everyone was subdued, even after we got to the farmhouse.

We gathered around the fireplace again. "I'll never forget the special times we've shared in this place," I said. I stood with my backside to the fire.

"We've loved it, too," Anna agreed. She was backed up to the fire beside me. She had her arm around my shoulders. "It's been one of the most special times of my life."

"Too bad it's got to end so soon," Clarence added. "There's word around camp that the train will be heading south to the winter quarters in a couple of days. That means we've really got to get serious about working out a plan, if we're going to help the hobos go free."

"It is so good of you to want to help those poor people," Aunt Mary said. "Goodness knows they could use some help. But before we get into all that, we have an idea we want to share with you." She paused and looked across at Uncle Cliff, where he stood leaning with his elbow on the mantle, puffing on his pipe. He nodded at her, so she continued.

"If you accept our idea, you won't have to go back there tonight, or ever again," she said softly. All three of us jerked around to look at her.

"What do you mean, Aunt Mary?" Edward asked.

She smiled that special kind of smile that looked so much like Mama when she had a reason to celebrate.

Uncle Cliff spoke up. "We've managed to get enough money together that we can buy three railway tickets—one for each of you—so you can go back home."

Clarence looked startled. "Why, that's mighty generous of you folks," he said.

I added, "It sounds so safe and easy. If we do that, we'll just never show up at the circus prison again, and they will have no way of tracking us down."

"It's hard t' believe that we can just hop on a real train, travel awhile, and be back home again," Edward said. He paused for a minute, then looked up at Aunt Mary. "Does this offer include dogs?" he asked, stroking Jiggs, who was in his lap.

"Yes," replied Aunt Mary, nodding her head. "It will be just that easy. And it does include dogs . . . and dolls," she added, smiling at me.

"This is mighty kind of you, Aunt Mary and Uncle Cliff," Clarence said. "Thanks a million for the wonderful offer."

"We appreciate it, more than you know." I looked around at the circle of smiling, expectant faces. The entire family sat silently around the room, giving us time to think about the offer that had just been made. Anna, holding her doll, winked at me.

I looked first into Clarence's eyes; then, Edward's. What I saw prompted me to continue my remarks.

"With all we've been through these past few days, though, you surely understand that we're not the only people involved here. Naturally, we're anxious to get home, but I just can't imagine going off and leaving Scottie, Joe, Ronald and the others without trying to help them get away, too."

I glanced back at Edward and Clarence, who both quickly nodded in agreement.

Uncle Cliff was taken aback. He said, "Come now, children. This is a brave thing for you to do. Brave and noble. But we're terribly concerned for your safety."

"Yes," Aunt Mary chimed in. "There's no telling what those dreadful people might do to you before this is all over. We *insist* on getting the tickets for you." She nodded her head to punctuate her remark.

But no matter how hard they tried, they couldn't convince us to take the easy way out. We were determined to try to free our fellow captives from their enslavement. "Can't you see?" I asked. "We believe we can help them see the light of freedom again."

When Aunt Mary saw our determination, she finally shook her head back and forth, shrugged her shoulders, and held out her hands with her palms up in a gesture of surrender. She said, "Even though I hate to see you go back to that frightful place, I'm proud of you for being so brave. You can count on us to help any way we can. Just promise me you'll put that warning bundle on the wall if you need *anything*."

Uncle Cliff slowly nodded his head in agreement. "That's right. If you need anything at all," he repeated.

In spite of the lateness of the hour, the entire family rode along to deliver us, one last time, to our prison home. We thanked them again for the hospitality they had shown us, and for all the love they had shared. With kisses all around, and last goodbyes, we crawled back through the hole in the brick wall, ready to face whatever awaited us.

CHAPTER 20

The next morning, as the five of us entered the mess hall for breakfast, we stopped dead in our tracks. Something had changed. It took less than a minute for us to realize what it was that seemed so different.

I exclaimed, "It's noisy in here. Can you believe it? They're talking! The wind-up toys are actually talking to each other."

Just at that moment, there was a burst of laughter from across the tent. With all of them talking and laughing, it was obvious that a change had come over the entire group.

"What d' ye think . . . " Scottie began.

Smokey Joe cleared his throat loudly. We all looked around at him. He was smiling smugly.

"Ain't it interestin' what a little change of flavorin' kin do to the meat," he grinned. "Been changin' the flavorin' fer several days, now."

"So that's what you've been up to," I said. "I knew you were doing more of the cooking, but I didn't know why until now."

"I may be slow, but I ain't dumb," Joe said. "Jist a matter of switchin' a few jars around. If the drug that slowed the bums down is left outta their food, then it seems only likely that they'd all start returnin' to normal in a matter of days. 'Specially when the drug's been dumped in the garbage."

My brothers and I winked at each other. It seemed to be working on humans, thanks to Smokey Joe. Hopefully, it would work on horses, as well.

Major Andrews and Sergeant Lorrie made their usual morning stopover at the mess hall during breakfast. They did not appear to be at all pleased with the change in their laborers' behavior. They shook their heads and frowned. As long as they were there, I made it a point to do my wind-up toy act with slow motion and dull-staring eyes. I noticed that Smokey Joe did the same.

When they left together, I went to the window and watched them go. They walked across the compound and out the main gate. As they climbed the steps in front of the big white house next to the prison, another tall man joined them. This time, the men were not laughing. Even across the distance of the compound, I could tell they had determined looks on their faces as they entered the door of the house.

I went back to work, washing the mountains of dishes. I was still thinking about the three men when I saw Anna coming in the main entrance with her usual basket of eggs and dairy products. My heart did a little flip as I realized this would be the last time I would see her under these circumstances. She had become, not just a distant relative, but my new best friend.

I dried my hands on the drying rag and rushed over to receive the supplies. We greeted each other with big smiles as we squeezed each other's hands.

"Emma Mae," she whispered, "is there any way you can come to the big top this afternoon for your brothers' show? Father is making arrangements for our whole family to go. We would love for you to join us."

"That's wonderful!" I replied. "I'll make it a point to be there."

"Great! We'll see you then." She picked up the empty basket and strolled quietly out the door. It was all I could do to contain my excitement as I trudged back to finish washing the pots and pans that still loomed beside my sink.

Since my job at the mess hall only lasted through midday cleanup, I hurried through my duties so I could be free by the two-o'clock show. I stood in the compartment of my tent, trying to decide whether to go to the show wearing my usual hobo outfit, or the nice boy outfit I had borrowed from my cousins. Even though my hobo clothes were quite soiled, I decided I'd wear them, after all.

When I got to the circus area, I made my way around to the back of the bleachers until I spotted our relatives. I crawled between the wooden benches until I got to the place where Anna was sitting. I squeezed through the open space she had saved beside her. They laughed when they saw me joining them from *beneath* the seats.

A boy sat at the opposite end of the bleachers that I didn't know, but Aunt Mary introduced us. "Emma Mae," she pointed to the boy, "this is Jimmy. His parents are the bareback riders here at the circus. Clarence brought him over to sit with us during the show."

Jimmy and I waved at each other excitedly.

"Aunt Mary, Uncle Cliff, I see Dr. Hess across the way," I said, pointing to a balding man with reddish-colored hair. He had his arm around a younger woman with long blond hair. Beside her sat two young men, also with light-colored hair. They were both quite handsome. I could imagine that they might one day have their own horse show in a circus. Uncle Cliff nodded at me and winked.

Just then the ringmaster walked to the center of the big top. Knowing what I did about Sergeant Lorrie, it made me feel strange to see him in this important role. He raised a megaphone to his mouth and shouted: "Ladeeeze and gen-tle-men! Welcome to our last full afternoon performance under the big top for this season. We hope you will enjoy your afternoon of entertainment. Now may I present . . . the most spectacular . . . circus . . . anyplace on earth!"

The musicians, sitting on risers in the center of the pavilion, immediately began to play. What a thrill to sit in this enormous tent and watch the parade as it entered through the opening across the way from where we sat. "Just look at all the animals," Anna yelled to me. Elephants lumbered along in their fancy decorations and costumed riders. Ostriches strutted and kangaroos hopped. Clowns did tricks as they moved around the spectator area.

"Look! Look! Here come Clyde and Dale, my favorite horse friends," I shouted over the music. As they pranced through the entrance to the tent, I saw they were pulling a fancy flatbed cart with . . . I couldn't believe my eyes . . . our very own clowns! Yes, Scottie was juggling, Edward was playing along with the band, and the two dancers were performing, even as they rode around the tent.

Behind the horses and cart, there was a tall lady giraffe. "Hey, everybody," I called. "Here comes Mama Giraffe, the one who saved me in the barn." I jumped up and down as I watched her walking along with her funny gait. She was wearing a lady's hat on her head, with a long scarf tied around her neck. As she held her head high, she appeared to be looking down her nose at the rest of us, as if she thought she was just a notch better than everybody else. Her baby giraffe scurried along beside her. It looked adorable in its baby bonnet.

When the parade ended, the circus itself began. The high-trapeze act was breathtaking, causing us to gasp and shiver with delight. The

lions and tigers were ferocious, but the tamers kept them all under control with the snapping of their whips.

How exciting it was when Jimmy's parents performed their daring acts of flips, whirls, and feats with the horses. Even though the horses themselves were not lively and spirited, the show, overall, was outstanding.

The audience applauded loudly when our clowns performed their routine of music, dancing, and juggling. I thought my heart would burst with pride when they got a standing ovation at the end of their act.

The rest of the show proceeded with its normal thrills and chills. I didn't want it to ever end, because I knew this would be my last encounter with our special family here in Wisconsin.

When it was over, our clowns joined us for a while, before they left to clean the elephants' stalls. They were delighted that these special members of our family had filled a section of the audience on the last day of the show.

Then, before Clarence and Edward left, Jimmy's parents came to meet all of us. They were especially pleased to get acquainted with Uncle Cliff and Aunt Mary. "We don't live far from you," his mother said. "Now that the circus duties are going to be cut back for the winter, Jimmy would enjoy having friends in the area. Do you think he could come to your farm to play with your children?"

"Of course, of course," Aunt Mary responded. "Matthew, Mark, and Luke, as well as the girls, are always glad to have friends come over to play. The rest of you are welcome, too, for that matter. Please come when you can."

As we lingered a bit longer, saying goodbye to our family, I looked up to see Major Andrews strolling our way. My heart skipped a beat. He stopped and looked at the group surrounding his prize performers, scowling. Question marks were written all over his face. I turned quickly away from him, talking to Anna and Johnna Mae about the show. Even though I didn't look directly at him, I could tell, out of the corner of my eyes, that he was looking at me through narrowed lids.

What was he thinking? Did he still resent me for stomping on his foot the first time we met? Why was he always watching me? Was he aware of our late-night activity? Did he wonder who this family was that surrounded us just now? Did he connect me with the "boy with the bad cold" he had met a few days ago? At that moment, I was glad I had chosen to wear my hobo clothes, instead of the other outfit. What a relief I felt when he turned and stalked away, shaking his head.

As I watched him go, I noticed another small group of people across the arena, deep in conversation. I realized it was Uncle Cliff talking to none other than Dr. Hess, Erina, and her brothers. I felt sure Uncle Cliff was making suggestions about possible places of employment for the young immigrants from Russia.

The clowns and Jiggs, with Jimmy in tow, went off toward the elephant stalls outside the big tent. The family said their last goodbyes and walked away, blowing kisses as they went. I was left behind on my own.

The big top was practically abandoned now. A few people were cleaning up, here and there. I sat in the middle of a section of bleachers, with my elbows on my knees and my chin in my hands. I tried to absorb the entire experience. I couldn't help but ask myself the same questions I had asked all along. Why would anyone in the world want to treat another person as a slave? How could some people use other people for their own gain? Why did some folks have good luck and some not so good? What did any of this mean . . . never again to see light?

Still not having answers, I rose from my seat, climbed down the empty benches of the now-vacant tent, and, with my hands in the pockets of my trousers, slowly walked away.

The golden and red leaves on the trees in the center of the complex danced in the slanted rays of the late afternoon sun. As the breeze lifted the swirling leaves that had already fallen to the ground, it also lifted my spirits.

Maybe there is light, after all, I thought. I smiled as I kicked the leaves in all directions. And, just maybe, we can still find it.

That night all five occupants of the blue tent, along with Ronald Wood, who dared to sneak into our place *after* Taps, stayed up and made plans. The lantern light wasn't blown out until just before dawn.

Chapter 21

Once again, Reveille came early. From the moment we stepped out of our tent to go to breakfast, we knew that change was in the air. The sky was heavy with low, gray clouds. Cold wind off Lake Michigan blasted across the campground and went straight through our lightweight clothing. We shivered in the cold.

We had just begun to walk toward the mess hall, when Major Andrews came hurrying through the main gate. He stopped in his tracks when he saw us, glaring spitefully. The five of us returned his angry stare. He looked around at the workers who had come up behind him. One hobo was pushing a wheelbarrow loaded with bricks. Another carried a shovel and a bucket filled with a grayish substance that looked like mortar.

"All right, men," Major Andrews directed the workers. "We're going around to the brick wall behind the mess hall where there's a *large* hole." He pointed with his finger. "We have a good idea about how it got there . . . " he glanced accusingly in our direction . . . "and, after what the night watchman witnessed in this area night before last, we have evidence that explains how it's gotten so big. When we get the hole closed up, once and for all, we'll work on punishing the persons responsible for it."

I shuddered as he glared with squinted eyes in our direction. I was glad he didn't look directly at our faces, because he might have noticed our looks of alarm at the news that our only escape route to the outside world was being shut off.

Major Andrews and his crew tromped off to carry out their task of repairing the hole in the wall. The three of us watched them go.

"What do you think?" Clarence asked, looking at Edward and me. "Should we put the red bundle on top of the wall?"

Ed and I nodded immediately. "From the way things sound," I said, "Major Andrews is not exactly happy with us. Plus, he's closing up our only way out of here."

Without saying another word, Ed disappeared inside the tent. He popped back out in no time, carrying the red hobo bundle, still tied onto its stick. He and Clarence hurried around behind the blue tent where Clarence boosted him up on his shoulders. Edward placed the bundle so that it hung over the wall on the outside. The barbed wire on top held it in place. We knew that Anna would notice the bundle hanging there when they arrived with the morning supplies.

After our signal for help had been placed on the wall, the rest of the group went on to breakfast. I stayed behind like we had planned, waiting for Anna. It seemed like hours passed before I finally saw her coming through the gate. I went darting over to meet her.

"Here," I said loudly, for the benefit of the guards. "I'll take the eggs to the kitchen from here. We're just about out of food this morning." I took the egg basket and bag of supplies from her. In the process, we grabbed each other's hands and squeezed. We both had tears in our eyes. I handed her our instructions.

"When we got near the camp," she whispered, "we saw the red bundle on the wall. Are you all right?"

I shrugged my shoulders. "We're safe enough right now, but they're closing up our escape hole this very minute. And the major looks pretty upset with us, so we don't know what he has in mind. We're sure the entire group will be leaving right after breakfast. Run and show our plans to your family. We've got to have your help. Hurry!"

I watched as she walked at a normal pace through the gate, breaking into a run just after she passed the guards. I knew we could count on them.

As it turned out, the timing for putting our plan into action couldn't have been better. When breakfast was over, Major Andrews appeared with his black megaphone. He had the men assemble outside the mess hall. This time the group was not subdued. As a matter of fact, it was just plain noisy.

"May I have your attention, please?" he barked into the megaphone. Instead of responding with silence, as had happened on the day of our arrival, the men continued talking and laughing.

Again he said, but louder, "May I please have your attention?" Still they kept talking, ignoring him.

We could see Sergeant Lorrie standing near the major, rapidly twirling his curly mustache. His shifty eyes darted from face to face around the noisy crowd. We smiled at the transformation that had come about as a result of Smokey Joe's new "recipe" for the meat.

Major Andrews, apparently, thought it was anything but funny. "All right!" he bellowed into the megaphone. "Quiet! I want to give you instructions!" This time the men gradually settled down to listen.

"Now that the weather is getting colder, the time has come for us to leave this camp for our winter quarters in Florida. Most of you have done this many times. As is our usual practice, when the train goes out, we all go. We will be picking up new volunteers along the way."

When he said that, I shivered, but not from the cold.

"General Rankin has brought the train back and is prepared to leave within the next hour. We will begin boarding right away. Just follow Sergeant Lorrie. He will show you where to go and tell you what to do."

Major Andrews took the megaphone down from his mouth.

From somewhere near the back of the group, someone shouted, "Why didn't we know about this before now?"

Someone else said, "What if we don't wanna go? You cain't make us."

Still another said, "We're gettin' sick and tired of Sergeant Lorrie tellin' us what to do!"

From somewhere in the group, one of the hobos began chanting: "We won't go! We won't go!" Then another person picked up the cry. "We won't go! We won't go!"

Gradually, the refrain was picked up as more of the men joined in. "We won't go!" The chant continued growing in volume.

The two officers looked at each other with widened eyes. Major Andrews turned and shouted one word into the megaphone. "GUARDS!" The two men with guns standing by the gate marched forward with their rifles lowered at the crowd. There was instant silence.

"Now!" the major spoke more quietly into the megaphone, "That's more like it. As always, you will do as you are told . . . or else! We'll be walking past yonder prison on the way, so I strongly suggest you follow orders. Understood?" He quietly scanned the downcast faces of the group in front of him. "We're ready to move to the station now."

One of the men in back called out, "I don't want t' go back to Florida. I hate it down there."

Major Andrews immediately turned to one of the guards and, in a loud voice, said, "Guard, I'm going to ignore that remark, but if anyone else has an opinion to express, you are to bind them up and take them to the prison. That's an order!"

The guard clicked his heels together and saluted, then aimed his rifle at the crowd again.

Sergeant Lorrie yelled, "All right, all of you. You know what to do. Follow me." The subdued men, including the lone protestor, looked at the rifles pointed in their direction, and began to follow.

We trailed behind at the back of the group. When we got near our blue tent, the boys darted behind it to get the hobo bundle off the wall. Then we rushed inside to retrieve our belongings.

I grabbed Maizey and wrapped her inside the blue velvet dress. My crumpled crown was in the corner of my compartment, so I grabbed that, too. At the last minute, I remembered to reach under my cot to retrieve the bundle of clothing I had borrowed from my cousins.

Edward picked Jiggs up, and Clarence got the lantern. The two boys collected all the clown costumes, including the ones that belonged to Scottie and Jiggs. Then we fell in line behind the others, looking around at the colorful circus tents one last time.

As we walked through the guard gate, we glanced over to the nearby trees. There stood our Wisconsin family, smiling and waving at us. They began strolling nonchalantly behind us at a safe distance. It was reassuring to know they were ready to help put our plan into action.

Even so, I was dreadfully nervous. So many things were going to have to fall into place, and at exactly the right time. Could we pull it off? I wondered. If we failed, would we, truly, be bound to this slave camp for the rest of our lives, along with this group of men?

Scottie and Smokey Joe walked up ahead, talking quietly to each other. I smiled when I recalled that, just last night, we had finally had our question answered about the incident in the woods on that long-ago Halloween evening.

It so happened that the two friends had been killing time that afternoon in the field of one of our rich neighbors, Mr. Singleton. They had each picked up a large stick and had playfully pretended to be having a sword fight.

They had no idea there was a cow in the field, but suddenly, from out of nowhere, a bull came charging at them with its head lowered. Although it appeared to be young and fairly small, it had sharp-looking, pointed horns. These were aimed right at Scottie!

Scottie grabbed a club-like stick from the ground and held it out, instinctively, to protect himself from the oncoming bull. The bull kept charging. Just as it got close enough to attack, Scottie swung the club in self-defense. He accidentally caught the bull right in its temple, and it fell down. Dead!

When they looked down at the dead animal, they recalled hearing stories about how proud Mr. Singleton was of his young, prize bull.

They knew, without a doubt, this must be that bull. They panicked! There was a rickety-looking wheelbarrow pushed up to the fence at the edge of the field. It was filled with tow sacks. A rusty shovel was propped against it.

Although it was a challenge, they pulled and tugged until they got the young bull into the wheelbarrow. They covered it with the burlap bags and went out in search of a place to bury it. Even though it had been an accident, they hadn't wanted Mr. Singleton to know what they had done.

They were surprised to learn that Edward and I had witnessed the first part of that burial from our secret hideout.

Why had they chased us on Halloween night? It was simply because they had wanted to find out who was in the woods that late at night. They had meant no harm to us whatsoever. We had laughed about the incidents last night, since we had become such good friends. I smiled now, remembering.

As I came out of my daydream, I realized we were walking past the white house and the castle-like prison. I had no way of knowing how many people were inside that prison, but seeing the armed guards marching back and forth in front of the gates made my skin prickly. How many innocent persons, I wondered, were prisoners there, simply because they had made an officer angry.

Out of the corner of my eye, I saw movement on the porch of the white house we had just passed. I looked back in time to see a tall man come out the front door. He stood, stiff and straight, watching the parade of hobos shuffling by. I had the feeling I had seen him someplace before, but I couldn't remember where.

Wait a minute! The tall man was wearing striped coveralls and a striped engineer's cap. Why, that had to be General Rankin, the ringleader of the operation. Just as that thought entered my mind, Major Andrews walked up the steps and saluted him. The general returned the salute.

We were almost out of hearing range by then, but I heard the major say, "General Rankin. The volunteers are prepared to board the train. We are almost ready for departure."

As I turned the corner, I heard the general's reply. "Very good, major. Carry on."

We were in sight of the train station by now. As we approached the tracks, I saw the outline of the train with its makeshift wooden cars. It looked the same as it had the day we arrived, except it was headed in the opposite direction. The doors of the train stood open. On down the line, a cloud of steam rose from the locomotive.

Major Andrews raised the megaphone to his mouth. Behind him, Sergeant Lorrie and the guards stood at attention. "All right, men," he bellowed. "You may now board the train."

Like wind-up toys once again, the men began to file onto the barely visible train. They looked beaten, defeated.

While the boarding was taking place, my mind wandered again. Last night we had finally learned the story about the general and his part in all of this. Ronald Wood told us the account of how the man known as General Rankin had been a fantastic magician as a young man. People all over the country had said that his feats of magic were some of the most incredible acts ever known. It was even thought that he might become one of the greatest magicians of all times.

Somewhere along the way, however, he let his fame and fortune go to his head. He got involved with the wrong people, stole a lot of money, and ended up spending many years in the penitentiary. After he had served his prison term, he found that he no longer had a place in the world of performing. Nobody would book his shows. He was an outcast.

It was then that he decided to take revenge. He developed his greatest achievement ever—a nearly invisible, disappearing train. He now used the train to take control of people's lives. He, along with the admiral and sergeant, were the owners of the circus as well as the train. By using hobos as slaves for all their operations, they were extremely wealthy.

Another blast of steam from the train's engine brought me out of my reverie, just in time to see the general as he walked stiffly down the platform. Uncle Cliff and Matthew strolled casually along behind him, following the general from a discreet distance. The bulge under Uncle Cliff's jacket told me they were ready for their part in the plan.

In front of me, Ronald Wood climbed aboard the crude-looking train with the others. Before he disappeared from our view, he lifted his hat and nodded at us. A quick wave of his hand with his finger and thumb forming a circle was the signal that everything was okay.

Smokey Joe also clambered aboard. Somewhere along the walk to the train, he had found a fresh cigar stub to stick in his mouth. He took it out now and waved it at us. He gave us a big wink. He was ready for his part in the plot.

All the men, under the watchful eyes of the guards, had quietly boarded the barely-visible train by now, except Scottie and the three of us.

"What are *you* waiting for?" Sergeant Lorrie asked, scowling at us as we hung back. "It's time for you trouble-makers to go, too."

We started moving toward the train when Major Andrews, who was standing near us on the platform, reached his arm out in front of me. "Everyone except *you*, missy," he said. He grasped me by the shoulders and bent over so that his face was directly in front of mine. His dark eyes glared at me. "And *you*, dear girl, or dear boy who sometimes wears a disguise, are headed straight for that prison yonder!" He narrowed his eyes even more and whispered in a hateful-sounding voice, "Never again to see light, my dear. Never again to see light!"

I stood glaring back into the eyes of the man in the brown suit with the black derby hat as he leaned down to my level.

This turn of events had caught me totally off-guard. My mind raced as I wondered how I was going to get out of this predicament. Then I saw movement out of the corner of my eye. It was Anna, right on cue, carrying a basketful of eggs. Scottie rushed over, grabbed some eggs from the basket, and started juggling.

The diversion worked. Both Sergeant Lorrie and Major Andrews whirled around to see what on earth Scottie was doing. While they stared at the man with the bushy red beard, juggling eggs in the middle of the train platform, Aunt Mary, Mark, and Luke, snuck up behind them, carrying burlap bags. Quickly, they pulled the bags over the heads of the unsuspecting men. This was the cue for Clarence and Edward to run back and help tie them up. Scottie stopped juggling eggs so that he, too, could help secure the ropes around the struggling men.

As the bag had been pulled down over Major Andrews' arms and hands, I had, thankfully, been set free. My sigh of relief was short-lived, though, because the two guards, who had stood by the gate to the compound every day since our arrival, came hurrying toward the struggle with their rifles raised. My heart stopped at the sight of them. At any second, I expected gunshots to ring out as they attempted to rescue the officers.

To my complete surprise, the guards looked at each other, then laid their guns down. They dashed the remaining distance across the platform to lend a hand in helping bind the struggling officers. With so many people working together, the sergeant and major were quickly bound to a lamppost, standing back-to-back, in the middle of the train station.

We were very pleased that the plan had worked so well, but were surprised when we heard loud cheering coming from the passengers on board the train. They were hanging out the windows, yelling their approval.

The guards briefly explained their actions. It seems they had hated the jobs they had been forced to do at the prison complex. One of them told us he had overheard our remarks in our tent a couple of nights ago about helping set the hobos free. He wanted to help, too, but didn't know how he could until today. They, too, were homeless men who had been picked up by General Rankin's mysterious train. Now they wanted to take a ride to freedom on the magical train that was barely visible there on the tracks.

Just then, there were four blasts on the train whistle—two longs and two shorts. This was our signal that the other part of the plan had been successful. It was time for us to hop aboard.

Anna and Johnna Mae rushed to my side. We hugged each other tightly in a three-way hug—four-way, including Maizey. "I'll never forget you, dear cousins," I cried, hugging them again. "Let's keep in touch by writing letters. Okay?" I said to Anna.

"By all means," she answered, "starting now." She placed a folded paper in my hand. I smiled and tucked it in my trousers, then handed her the bundle of boy clothes I had brought with me.

"Hurrry up, childrrren," Scottie called excitedly, as he jumped aboard the train "It's time forrr us to go."

As the three of us and the two guards ran toward the train, we called out, "*Auf weidersehen*, Aunt Mary. Goodbye, everybody." The train slowly began to move forward. Then, just as there was a loud escape of steam from the locomotive, I couldn't resist it. It seemed like something told me to do it! I abruptly stopped running, turned, and dashed back to a lamppost in the center of the train platform where two brown pants legs stuck out from beneath a burlap bag, and I did it! I stomped on his foot!

Major Andrews yowled and tried to grab his foot, but he couldn't because his arms were bound to the post.

"Who's not seeing light now, Major?" I shouted. "Who will never again see light?" I turned and ran back toward the train, as it was picking up speed.

"Come on, Emma Mae," Edward hollered from the open door of the train. "Hurry! Hurry!" He and Clarence pulled me up the steps, just as the door closed.

I looked through an open window for one more glimpse. Aunt Mary had her handkerchief over her mouth. She was crying and waving, as her niece and nephews moved down the tracks and out of her life.

The train was moving faster now. We passed Uncle Cliff and Matthew, waving and grinning broadly. Standing with them was a balding man with reddish hair. It was Dr. Hess, the veterinarian. In the center of this group there was a tall man, wearing striped coveralls. A burlap bag was tied over his head and upper body. Obviously, General Rankin, the ringleader of this operation and an incredible magician, would not be able to pull a magic trick out of *this* bag!

When I saw them there, I had a flashback. Night before last, as Uncle Cliff was about to leave us at our hole in the wall, he promised he would get Dr. Hess to help him handle the entire situation of turning these people over to the authorities. He said they would also get the innocent captives released from prison right away. There would be no more people kept against their wishes, ever again.

"Thanks, Uncle Cliff and Matthew," we cried as the train moved past them, rushing down the tracks.

"Good luck to you and Erina, Dr. Hess!"

"*Danke*! *Auf wiedersehen*! Goodbye!"

CHAPTER 22

The three of us, along with Scottie, walked through the rickety aisles of the train cars. The men on board were talking pleasantly among themselves instead of sitting in silence, as they had done on our first trip.

It was interesting that I no longer thought of these men as hobos, but as friends. Each one had his own story about what had brought him to this way of life. Hopefully, after this experience, each had gained a little glimmer of hope and a fresh outlook.

When we got to the front of the train, we found Smokey Joe operating the steam engine like a professional. He was wearing General Rankin's engineer's hat and a big grin.

"Looka here," he said, "Jist like m' old man used ter do. And I jist remembered somethin'. I don't git motion sick when I'm at the front o' the train. It's bein' a passenger that has always bothered me." He let Edward pull the chain that blew the whistle. In the broad open daylight, with Joe at the controls, it didn't sound eerie at all.

Ronald Wood now joined us. "I've explained to the passengers that they have the option of staying on the train and officially joining the circus in Florida, or getting off at the place of their choosing along the way," he said. "Many of them want to get off and try starting their lives over again. Here's a list of places where people want to stop."

He handed the list to Joe.

Scottie stroked his bushy red beard. "Me thinks I'll have ye add me name to the list forrr stopping in Chicago."

"ChiCAgo?" the three of us asked in unison.

"We thought you never wanted to go back to that ugly place again as long as you lived, Mr. Scottie," Edward said.

"Well, everrr since we talked about the grreat firre and me terrrible loss, I've been thinkin' 'bout it," he said. "Me thinks it might be good forrr me to face up to me fate and get a frresh start on me life. I've heard that they 'ave many a show where an old juggler like meself can make a decent livin'."

"Good for you, Scottie!" Clarence said, patting him on the back. "Here's the clown outfit you wore at the circus. It just might come in handy in your new career." He handed Scottie the bundle of clothing.

"We'll miss seeing you around our neighborhood," I said, hugging him tightly, "but maybe you can hop a train now and then and come back to Kentucky to pay us a call."

"That I'll do, me bonny lass and laddies," he smiled. "And thanks again forrr being friends to this old Scotchman. I'll never forrrget ye as long as I live. That, I won't."

"We'll never forget you, either, Mr. Scottie," Edward said, pumping his hand up and down in a big handshake.

Ronald, Wood was still acting as the train conductor. He had removed his coat and hat as he busily walked back and forth through the cars, checking on things. It seemed as though we hadn't been traveling long when he called out: "First stop, Chicago! All out for Chicago!"

The train slowed to a stop right in the middle of the big city with skyscrapers all around. This time we had an excellent view! A large number of men got off the train. They waved goodbye as they walked away toward their new lives.

The Scotchman with red hair and a bushy red beard also hopped off. He had a spring in his step and a determined look on his face as he waved goodbye, Joe blew the whistle, and we were off again.

After that, we stopped frequently, allowing the ex-prisoners to get off at the places of their choosing.

When we got near the stop where Ronald was to get off, he joined us once more in the engine of the train. He had put his jacket and hat back on. He looked at each of us, peering over the top of his glasses like he always did.

I said, "How can I feel happy and sad at the same time, Ronald?"

"That's the way I feel, too, Mr. Ronald," Edward chimed in. "Happy that you'll be back with your family, but sad because we'll be missin' you."

Ronald tousled Edward's hair and gave me a hug. "I know what you mean. I've become very fond of you children, but my own youngsters are some of the most important things in the world to me. It will be wonderful to be home with them again. I'll be free to enjoy my normal life once more."

Clarence remarked, "You're the reason why we're free. You helped us understand our situation and gave great advice about what to do." He pumped Ronald's hand up and down. "We'll always be grateful to you."

The train came to a complete stop. Ronald Wood practically jumped down the steps to the ground. Steam escaped from the engine, the whistle blared, and the train began to move forward. Our last glimpse of Ronald was of one happy schoolteacher, waving good-bye as he hurried down the tracks, returning home to his family.

We traveled through the day and into the night. Now that things had settled down, we were able to relax in the one nice car just behind the engine. When it grew dark outside, the gaslights in the windows surrounded us with a warm glow. The seats were soft and velvety. There were goodies to nibble on. We were traveling first class this trip!

I went into the one private compartment and changed my clothes, putting on the blue velvet dress. I twisted my hair and pinned it on top of my head. As I rolled the shirt and trousers into a bundle, I felt something bulky in the pocket of the pants. Why, it was the note that Anna had handed me as I was telling her goodbye. I had forgotten all about it.

I sat down in one of the plush seats, with a gaslight above it, to read my letter. At the top of the page, she had, once again, sketched in a design of ivy and flowers. Then she had written in her neat handwriting:

"Here are some little rhymes which I hope will help you remember me. I will never forget you, my dear cousin, Emma Mae.

'Tis sweet to meet
But sad to part,
I'll remember you
As a real sweetheart.

Remember me in sunshine,

Remember me in sorrow,
Remember me today,
And think of me tomorrow.

When I am far away
And my face you cannot see,
Take your pen and paper,
And write a line to me.
                    —Anna"

I sat thinking about my cousin for a while. I had never met anybody so like myself in almost every way. I felt sure we would have a regular correspondence in the future.

Just before it was our turn to get off the train in West Kentucky, we went to say one last goodbye to our dear friend, Engineer Smokey Joe.

"So you're taking the train all the way to Florida?" I asked. "When do you think you'll be coming back to this part of the country?" I had a lump in my throat at the idea of saying goodbye.

"I've allus wanted to see Floridy," he said. "If'n I likes it there, I might jist stay—except fer quick trips to visit m' friends once in a'while."

He cut his eyes around at us and said, in an apologetic voice, "When ye git a chance, I'd like to ask ye to go over to Mr. Singleton's place an' tell 'im about the bull. Scottie and me never meant to hurt 'im, much less kill 'im. Jist tell 'im we're awful sorry. An' nixt time I'm in town, whatever money I owes 'im for the loss of the bull, I'll settle up with 'im then."

"We'll be happy to do that, Mr. Joe," Edward responded. "But first we'll tell him that the 'willer-de-wisp tole you to. . . the willer-de-wisp tole you to.'"

The laughter that followed that remark helped chase away my tears. Joe was still smiling as we left him there, obviously enjoying a dream come true.

It wasn't long before we began to recognize familiar landmarks in our own part of the world. We were almost home. "Slow down, Smokey Joe," Clarence called. "We need to get off this train and go home to bed."

Joe slowed the engine . . . slower, slower, slower . . . until we stopped, right at the marshy bog where we had seen the will-o'-the-wisp. We jumped off the train, waving goodbye to Joe and the other remaining members of the former circus group. Joe couldn't resist making one last blast with the whistle as he waved out the window. I blew him a final kiss.

Without a sound, the almost-invisible train began to move away. It gradually picked up speed; then went swooping off in the darkness, swooping off in the night. The red light on the rickety caboose grew smaller and smaller, until it left our sight. When it was gone, there was nothing left but the silence.

As we stood there in that silence, beside the tracks, a brisk breeze blew across the marsh. The moon rode low in the western sky. Lightning bugs flashed in the treetops; but nothing interrupted the silence. Then, still holding on to the silence, we crossed the tracks and headed for home.

CHAPTER 23

A sense of unspoken closeness surrounded us as we trudged up the small hill on the opposite side of the tracks.

I put the crumpled paper crown back on my head, and tucked my shirt and trousers into a bundle under my arm. The blue eyes on Maizey's porcelain face stared at me in the moonlight.

Clarence and Edward rolled their clown outfits into bundles, as well. They adjusted their regular Halloween costumes so that they looked the same as they had when we left the Halloween party, oh, so many nights ago. Edward put his captain's cap back on, before taking Jiggs' clown hat off his head.

As we walked past the sweet potato cellar that was built into the hillside near the railroad tracks, Clarence suggested that we stuff my bundle of clothing and their clown costumes in the cellar for the night. He said he would put them in a better hiding place tomorrow. We stashed the clothes and closed the cellar door before moving on down the path in the direction of the house.

It was precisely at this moment that the strangest thing happened! I suddenly had an overwhelming feeling that maybe we hadn't been gone at all! When I said this to my brothers, they said they had the same feeling.

"But it did happen," I said emphatically. "I know it did. We have our clothes and costumes to prove it. The question is, are we going to tell anybody about it?"

"Do you think they would believe us?" Edward responded. He scratched above his left ear like he always did when he was not sure about something.

"I know *I* wouldn't believe us," Clarence added.

"Why don't we keep our secret to ourselves, then?" I asked. "We each have our own special things to help us remember."

"I won't need any help. I'll always . . . just remember." Ed whispered those last words with feeling.

We continued to walk toward the back door of our wonderful little farmhouse in Kentucky. Jiggs ran ahead and began to bark. He was barking at Maggie, my cat, who was sitting by a Jack-o-Lantern with a deliciously scary face. It was perched there on the backdoor steps, its candlelight gleaming brightly in the darkness. Why, it *was* still Halloween night!

We trooped into the house to find Mama sitting at the kitchen table, reading by the light of the coal oil lamp. She looked up and smiled fondly at her three spooks. "Did you have a good time at the party?" she asked. "I was waitin' up for you. I've been re-readin' this letter I got recently from my sister who lives in Wisconsin."

She shook her head wistfully. "I sure would love to go see her and her family. Would you believe it, they have children just about the same ages as you. Maybe someday we'll have a chance to go up there and visit them."

We all just looked at each other.

"We'd like that, Mama," I said, giving her a big hug. "I know Aunt Mary and Uncle Cliff must be wonderful people."

"*Ja,*" Clarence agreed, "wonderful people. And I'll bet their big dairy farm would be a great place to visit."

Edward yawned. "Maybe someday we can go up there in a *real* train and visit Anna and all the others."

Mama looked at me. Then, with a puzzled look on her face, she looked at both the boys. Finally, she looked at the letter in her hand and scratched her head. She stood and picked up the lamp. "Well, I don't know what you children have been up to, but I know you need to get to bed now. We need to call it a night."

"Wait a minute, Mama," I said, as she started toward my room. "There's something I want to ask you. Why did you tell Ed and me that you were worried about hobos being in the neighborhood when we got home from school today?"

"Oh, that. Those two friendly hobos who come around here a lot, Scottie and Smokey Joe, were here after breakfast this morning. They gathered that pile of pumpkins that's out by the well shed in the backyard. That red headed one actually carved the Jack-o-Lantern that's out on the back steps. I fried them some eggs and gave them some leftover greens and cornbread from last night's supper before they left."

She paused for a minute, thinking about the situation. "I guess I was a little uneasy about you two youngsters going to the Halloween party for the first time, and I was afraid there might be other hobos or pranksters around, trying to stir up trouble. I reckon, since mamas like me love their children so much, they sometimes worry about things that never even happen. I shouldn't have even mentioned it. I'm sure you didn't meet up with any other hobos during the night."

The three of us just exchanged smug grins when she made that last comment. Then the boys each gave Mama goodnight hugs and left to go to their bedroom. As they left the circle of lamplight, I saw they had their arms draped around each other's shoulders.

I picked my cat up in one arm and carried my doll in the other. Mama followed me into my own small bedroom, bringing the coal oil lamp. She helped me out of the heavy velvet dress. After unpinning my hair and shaking it loose, I slipped into my nightshirt and crawled between the covers on my very own feather bed. Maggie jumped on the bed and curled up at my feet. It felt so good to be home.

Mama stroked my hair, then leaned over and kissed me on the cheek. "I'm glad you had such a good time at the party."

"You'll never know what an unbelievable experience this Halloween has been," I said sleepily as I closed my eyes, "or how glad we are to be free."

Mama looked a bit puzzled when I made that remark, but she said, "Get a good night's sleep, now. *Gute Nacht*, my little *Fraulein*." She carried the lamp with her as she tiptoed from my room.

"*Danke, Mutter. Gute Nacht.*"

As darkness filled the space around me, my eyelids closed. I was almost asleep, to dream of speeding trains, circuses, and a wonderful place called home, when an idea popped into my head. My eyes popped open! I sat straight up in bed!

If this unbelievable adventure happened on the tracks, I thought, I wonder . . . could something else magical happen at another time and in another place? Hmmm.

I lay back down and closed my eyes, this time drifting off to sleep . . . with a smile on my face.

THE END ?

CPSIA information can be obtained at www.ICGtesting.com
Printed in the USA
LVOW06s1451030314

375855LV00008B/111/P